i ≠
L579s

A SEASON FOR UNICORNS

SONIA LEVITIN

A
SEASON
FOR
UNICORNS

Atheneum   1986   New York

Library of Congress Cataloging-in-Publication Data

Levitin, Sonia
A season for unicorns.

SUMMARY: Disillusioned by her father's infidelity,
Inky abandons her family to seek courage and honesty in
a household operating a hot air balloon launch.
[1. Hot air balloons—Fiction. 2. Family problems—
Fiction] I. Title
PZ7.L58Se   1986   [Fic]   85-20051
ISBN 0-689-31113-3

Published simultaneously in Canada by
Collier Macmillan Canada, Inc.
Composition by Heritage Printers,
Charlotte, North Carolina
Printed and bound by
Fairfield Graphics, Fairfield, Pennsylvania
Designed by Mary Ahern
First Edition

For Laurie Cherman,

my friend and believer,

and

For Susan Rubin,

with love.

A SEASON FOR UNICORNS

1

WHEN I WAS very young, even before my little sister Becca was born, I used to climb to the top of the tall slide at the children's playground in San Diego. My father took a photograph of me standing on the highest rung of the ladder, grinning—*no hands!* Mother knelt at the bottom, looking worried.

Afterward, Daddy took me on the ferris wheel at the park. I absolutely loved it. I wasn't afraid of heights then. Funny, how people change. When did it happen? I can't remember, except that by the time I was in second grade I stayed off the jungle gyms and out of trees; I preferred painting at the easel and making turtles out of clay. I also had a little boyfriend, Joey Sherwood. I mention this to prove I'm not afraid of boys or of getting close, even though that is probably what Buzz Duarte has been telling everyone. He called me frigid. It isn't true.

I'd been watching Buzz all summer at the pool. When I say "pool," don't imagine anything fancy. Seven Wells is an old railroad town, population 1400, right at the edge of the desert. We have a beat up old municipal pool where all the kids go to keep cool in the summertime. It gets hotter than blazes here, as my father says.

We moved to Seven Wells because of Grandma. She couldn't live alone anymore and needed the dry, desert heat for her asthma. So my father sold her tiny house and bought one just a little larger in the same town, where we could all live together.

Mother loves Seven Wells. She says it reminds her of home in Nebraska. Mom never did like San Diego, with its traffic and the constant stream of vacationers. My father's a pilot. He flies out of San Diego, which is nearly two hours away. He's on three days, off three or four, so he doesn't mind the commute.

All summer at the pool, Krista, Barbara, Caroline, and I watched the boys. Krista and Barbara are best friends, like me and Caroline. We each had our own idol. Mine was Buzz Duarte. Watching boys was nothing new; we'd been doing it for years, but now we were fourteen. This was our last summer before high school, and I'd never had a real date before. Oh, we all hang out together at Peaches, the ice cream store, but you know what I mean. When Buzz Duarte asked me to the

Chamber of Commerce end-of-summer hayride, I was excited. It was going to be the best night of my life. That was two weeks ago, exactly. Now, when I think about it, I want to die.

The date was a disaster. It wasn't during the hayride; that was great. But afterward, when we got to the old ranch house where they had food and dancing, kids started going off in couples, and Buzz and I, dancing, began to kiss.

We have been goofing off playing kissing games like Truth or Dare since we were eleven. This was different. The way he held me, the way I felt—a sinking, floating, falling feeling—was absolutely delicious and exciting. I'd never been kissed that way. My whole body felt different, sort of electrified. Every time I tried to breathe, I felt it more and more.

As we kissed, Buzz led me outside, and then we were behind the huge barn with bushes and haystacks concealing all but the tender moonlight. We could hear the music from the stereo, feel the night softness; something melted in me, and when his hands began to move over my body, I had no will, no control, only that plunging feeling of desire going wild. It erased all other thoughts from my mind, all other feelings from my body.

I'll never know what came over me, but suddenly I jerked away from him, hauled off, and with all my might socked Buzz Duarte right in the stomach.

Buzz Duarte doubled over. His face went white. He

looked at me as if I were a snake and croaked out in a strange voice, "What's wrong? What'd I do? Are you crazy?"

I ran. Later, when the trucks were ready to leave again, Buzz followed me at some distance. We were silent all the way home. Stiffly Buzz walked me to my door, still guarding himself.

"Good night," he said. He made a face. "Keep in touch."

Mortified, I ran inside. I called out to my mother, who inquired from the bedroom, "Did you have a good time?" Then I huddled under the covers, awake most of the night.

In the morning my father wanted to know all about my big date. "Inky, baby, did you have fun?" Nobody calls me by my real name, Ingrid, except at school.

"Oh, yes, it was fabulous." I couldn't stand to think about it.

"When I was a kid, we used to neck all night in the hay," my dad said, grinning. He gave me a huge hug and a wet, smacking kiss. I wiped it off with my hand and moved stiffly aside.

"What's wrong, princess? Oh, I get it. Your old dad's been replaced," he said with a laugh. "Fair enough. But do ya love me just a little?" He winked, making his monkey–clown face, and I smiled in spite of myself.

When Caroline called, I said I couldn't talk. How could I tell her what had happened when I didn't really know myself?

That was two weeks ago. I still got chills whenever I saw Buzz Duarte, which was every day, because we were in the same English class. We never speak. He looks right through me. There was no way I could avoid him, especially if I was going to get involved in school activities.

The four of us had decided we'd really get involved this last year. Caroline and Krista were going out for song girls; Barbara already played saxophone in the band. They all decided I should try out for Roadrunner.

The Roadrunner, a desert bird, is our team mascot. We have this fabulous costume, with an enormous head and pointed beak, feathered body, and floppy rubber claws. Somebody's father used to work at Disney Studios and got the costume there. You have to be fairly tall to wear it. I tried on the costume a week ago and it fit. Not only that, it did something to my spirit. Inside that costume I leapt and clowned around, dancing and miming. My friends cheered and clapped. "You'll be perfect, Inky! You'll be the best Roadrunner ever!"

I grinned. "O.K. I'll do it." Actually, it felt terrific to play a part, to be rid of restraint.

The afternoon of the tryouts the bleachers were already crammed with kids when Caroline and I arrived. Castle Junior High School really has spirit. Everyone comes to the events, even the little kids. Sounds of horns and drum beats came from the band area. People laughed and screamed. The microphone hummed out its buzzing sounds. I felt hot and sticky, queasy and a little scared about trying out in front of all those people. Caroline pulled my arm. "Guess who's trying out for announcer?"

"Who cares?"

"You'll care, if you dare." Caroline has this silly way of making rhymes. It can be either funny or maddening.

The announcer is in charge of all the pep activities, including Roadrunner's antics. Right now, all I cared about was getting it over with, wondering whether I could really stand to walk around in that heavy head-piece. Would they all be laughing at me or with me? I began to shiver in spite of the heat.

"He'll make it for sure," Caroline continued, pulling me over to the bleachers, looking for seats. There were none, except at the very top. I don't like to sit way up there, having to climb up between those gaping slats.

I saw him then, standing with Coach Stanley at the microphone, wearing light beige cords and a pale plaid shirt, looking great, with that great smile of his. Buzz.

"Buzz Duarte!" exclaimed Caroline. "He'll make it. He's perfect. And if you make Roadrunner, won't that be neat? You and he can be together at all the events. You'll be a team. Ain't that a scream?"

I shook my head, feeling faint. From the very top of the bleachers Barbara and Krista waved and shouted; they were saving seats for us.

"What's wrong, Inky? You look sick."

Coach Stanley came toward me with the costume in his hands. "You trying out for Roadrunner? You want to go first?"

I heard Caroline shout back at Barbara and Krista. Her voice sounded hollow. I felt funny. Something I'd eaten, maybe; the taco I had for lunch seemed to be caught midway in my chest. I felt choked, dizzy. It was similar, somehow, to that moment at the hayride, before I socked Buzz Duarte—that panic.

"Hey, Roadrunner!" somebody called, and in the next instant something came down over my head. I gasped for breath, smelling that musty rubbery thing, and found myself in darkness—the mask was on backwards, pressing tight.

I yelled. My smothered voice and hot breath came back to me. I heard laughter out there. "Hey, Roadrunner! Can't catch me!" A hard smack came down against my back, knocking my breath away. Voices clattered, laughter beat around my head like the shrill shrieking in the fun house. Everything was dark and crazily spinning. I struck out, pushing and kicking. I tugged at the headpiece until finally I pulled it off and flung it down to the ground.

"Inky! What's the matter with you?" Caroline screeched.

I shouted back over my shoulder. "I have to go home."

"Inky, please wait. I'll help you. Won't you come back? Inky, Inky, please. It'll be so great if you're Road-runner!"

"I can't!" I screamed. "Leave me alone."

I prayed my father would be home. He'd come and

pick me up. Please, please, I murmured as I dialed our number from the pay phone, let him be there. Let him come for me. Mom would never drive to Castle by herself. She'd make me stay there and wait for the bus, and if I had to stay in that crowd one minute longer, I'd die.

The telephone rang and rang. My lips were beginning to go numb, my hands tingled. At last an answer—my father's voice. I wept and begged him to come for me.

"Baby, of course I will. You wait right there. I'll come and get you."

At last he came driving up. I slipped into the car, leaned back against the cool leather upholstery.

"Drive!" I said desperately. "Oh, please drive. Let's get out of here."

My father said gently, "Take it easy, sweetheart. What happened? Aren't you feeling well?"

"I feel awful."

"Sick?"

"I don't want to go out there in front of all those people."

He patted my hand. "Who ever said you had to? You don't have to be Roadrunner, jumping around letting people laugh at you."

"You said it would look good on my record," I mumbled, crying.

"Come over here, Inky–Dinky." He drew me close, gave me a squeeze. "You don't have to do any of that silly stuff. Listen, let's you and I go home and take a bike ride up to the center. We'll stop for ice cream. How about it?

And, hey, I brought you a little something from Portland. Want to guess what it is?"

"Oh, Daddy," I moaned.

"Perfume. You're getting to be a young lady. Young ladies need perfumes and pretty things. Let me see that pretty face. Let me see you smile. That's my girl."

I thought, who cares about Roadrunner and those screaming, rowdy kids, about Buzz Duarte, and that crazy stuff at school. It's something I ate, just something I ate. But it doesn't matter. I don't have to do it. Daddy's going to take me home.

2

HOME WAS A HAVEN, quiet and cool. The front porch was shaded by trees, and so were the sides; leafy vines brushed the screens, growing against the windows of Grandma's room. Hers was a long and narrow room that used to be a sun porch. From it, we usually heard Grandma's rocking chair creaking and the low sound from her little TV. Today it was comforting. I was home.

Father called out as we entered. "Marguerite! Here she is. Your princess is home safe. Just a little tired, I guess. Too much rough stuff."

Mother came out wearing her cotton robe and scuffs. I could tell she had been "lounging," as she calls it, spending the afternoon on her bed with magazines piled around her, and two pillows propped under her back.

"Does she have a fever?" Mother looked worried.

"I think she needs a double scoop ice cream cone," said my father, laughing. "We're going to ride on over to the center. Want anything?"

"Well, if you think she's up to it." My mother wrung her hands fretfully. "Are you sure you're all right, Inky? I could call Dr. Henry."

"She's fine, Marguerite," my father said sternly. His eyes glinted, a dangerous sign.

"Well really, Peter, if the child is so ill that you had to go all the way over to Castle to pick her up . . . ."

"I said she's fine. Are you contradicting me? Why do you contradict me in front of the children? What are they to think?"

The pulse throbbed at the side of his throat. One moment more and all would be lost, his jolly mood, the promise of a bike ride and that laughter we always shared when we went out together.

"Daddy!" I called out, making my voice merry. "Let's go. I'll race you. The winner has to buy the ribbons!" We had planned, last time, to buy bright ribbons for the handlebars of our bikes; my father had seen them somewhere. He loves colorful things.

"You're on, princess," he said with a sudden grin, and we pedaled on into town, past Dryer's Mortuary, past the Lucky Seven Motel, over to the six-block section called Main Street, with its flat-roofed little shops, all cluttered inside, the wares looking as if they, too, were beaten down from the heat. We crossed in accord

over to Fallon Street, that new addition people in Seven
Wells called "The Mall," in deference to the single covered arch that connected two long, low buildings housing
various modern stores. The new mall made the old timers
of Seven Wells proud. McClure's General Store boasted
gleaming front windows, shining chrome fixtures, and
wide counters filled with wares kept fresh by bright
lights and an air-conditioning system that worked all
year round. Beside the general store there were a couple
of clothing shops, a pharmacy, Peaches Ice Cream Par-
lor, and then a low office building.

We skidded over to the ice cream shop, laughing and
shouting, for we had raced hard the last block or two,
and of course, my father had won. He always won.

Inside, we stood at the counter, and Daddy nodded
toward the girl in her candy stripe uniform. "Look at
her," he said, without lowering his voice. "She's a real
cutie."

As if for the first time, I watched him, both joking and
intense. I could smell the Old Spice aftershave, noticed
how cool and clean he looked, even after bike riding, his
skin tanned and his hair crisp.

As the girl leaned over, her short skirt came up to re-
veal too much thigh. She walked toward us, red faced,
smiling flirtatiously. "What can I do for you today?"

"What would you like to do?" My father laughed.

"Scoop up some ice cream for you," said the girl play-
fully. She was much older than I, certainly out of school.
"What flavor?"

"Why don't you choose for me, dear," my father said. "Let's see what she'll pick." He nudged my arm.

"I'll have pistachio on the bottom and chocolate on top," I said, my usual order.

"You heard the lady. Be a dear, and give my girlfriend, here, a couple of extra big scoops."

"Your girlfriend, eh?" The girl laughed. She fluffed out her skirt, walked with a rippling gait.

"Yup. I like 'em young."

"Daddy," I whispered. "Please."

"What's wrong, honey. Can't you take a joke?"

The girl returned with our ice cream cones.

"What's this?" asked my dad.

"Maple nut and almond fudge. Nuts." Unabashed, the girl met his gaze.

For a moment the anger flickered in his eyes. Then instantly he brightened, throwing back his head, laughing. "Nuts to me, right? I guess I deserved that. Pardon me, I didn't mean to make you feel uncomfortable."

"No problem, sir."

"No harm in a little teasing, eh?"

"No problem."

"You're a real cutie. Next time you fly, look me up."

"Oh!" The girl's eyes grew wide. "You're a pilot?"

"Sure am. Maybe I'll have the privilege of taking you up someday. Here's a card. They'll give you a courtesy bus ride."

"Why, thank you!" The girl put the card into the little pocket in her red-and-white striped blouse. She looked very pleased, as if she had just met a celebrity, and she gave me a wink. *What a guy*, said the wink.

We browsed through the general store and bought ribbons for our bikes. My father talked to the clerks, telling a joke or two. They all knew him and called out, "Hey, Peter! How's it going?"

The town itself seemed to expand and deepen under my father's touch; he discovered things I never noticed when I was alone. People responded to him, coming alive and friendly. And he included me in the adventure. I bought two new charcoal pencils. As the clerk wrapped them, my father told her, "Inky, here, is a wonderful artist, did you know that? She paints beautiful pictures. You should see."

We went to the pharmacy to look around. Same thing. "So what's new, Harry? How's business?"

Harry, overweight and always sweating, confessed his failure with the latest diet. Dad sympathized, then drew me in.

"This girl can cook an omelette you wouldn't believe. Come over to the house some Sunday morning, she'll make you an omelette you'll never forget."

"You're a lucky guy, Peter."

"Yes, she's a terrific kid. Not like some of those rowdy ones. Takes good care of her little sister, too. And Becca adores her."

"Daddy," I whispered. "Please."

"What? Isn't it true? You're one heck of a kid." He smiled, put his arm around my shoulder with a squeeze.

"I should stop bragging, especially when you're around. Well, well, better than having kids you can only complain about, right, Harry?"

"You bet your life," agreed Harry the pharmacist. "We see 'em in here, come off the road on motorcycles, got purple hair, metal chains around their waists. You wouldn't believe it."

"We'd better get home, princess. Let's bring your Grandma some strawberries. You know how she loves them."

We rode over to the supermarket and picked out two baskets of strawberries and brought them home, laughing and singing out, "Berry time! Berry time!"

"Oh, Peter." Grandma smiled at her son, her pale blue eyes watering with emotion. "And you even brought whipping cream. My dear."

Becca came out, leaping into Daddy's arms, for she hadn't seen him since his last trip, and he'd been a whole week this time. "Hey, how's my little darling!" He scooped her up in his arms and began to tickle, until Becca screamed and begged for mercy. Then he gave her a tiny bottle of perfume, similar to mine, but much smaller, and a small glass unicorn. Becca collects unicorns.

"Oh, Peter, you do spoil them," murmured my mother, but her voice was warm with happiness. Her gift was a pale green quilted jacket with frog fasteners. She wore it now, queenly and proud.

"Nothing's too good for my girls," he said, looking at

each of us—Mother, me, Becca, and Grandma—smiling fondly.

I look back on that moment. In my mind we are like figures in a picture, posed inside a frame. We would never be that way again.

3

DADDY HAD BEEN gone for a whole week, and when he gets home from a long stint, we generally do something special. But Becca was working on a diorama, and he had promised to help her build a wooden box for it, covered with green carpeting to resemble a forest glade. The central character in this display was, of course, a unicorn.

I say "of course," because Becca has this passion for unicorns. She believes they really exist, which is kind of weird for a ten-year-old. Becca thinks she'll see a real unicorn some day, the way Caroline and I hope to see Bruce Springsteen live.

In addition to this diorama, Becca was working on a report about unicorns, gathering stories and legends. My father encouraged Becca's belief in unicorns. He also helped her to believe in Santa Claus much longer than most kids do. You'd think he'd want her to grow up. Anyhow, mother was reading magazines, Grandma was listening to TV and knitting, Becca and my father were making the diorama, and I was allowed to have Caroline over, not to fool around, but to do homework together. We hurried into my room, turned on the stereo, low, and sat down on the floor, our backs against the bed.

"So what really happened to you today?" Caroline nibbled on an apple. "You really freaked out."

"Did Buzz make it for announcer?"

"He's in the runoffs. So many kids were trying out for everything that we have to have two more tryout days, Coach Stanley said. The top guys will announce the next two games."

"You mean the final announcer won't be chosen for a month?"

"Yeah. But so what? It will give everyone else more time to practice."

"I'm not going to go for it," I said. I opened my carton of grape ade, the only drink we're allowed at home besides milk.

"Oh, Inky, you'd be fabulous. Three guys tried out today. None of them were as good as you."

"Caroline, I felt as if I was going to die inside that headpiece. It's hot. I couldn't breathe."

"You'd get used to it," Caroline said, taking another large bite from her apple. She leaned toward me. "Everybody's scared to get up in public like that. My mom said so. She used to perform on piano, you know. She was scared at first, too."

"Well, I wasn't scared. I just don't want to be Roadrunner."

"But we all talked about it, Inky! You'd be so perfect. And you'd get to be with Buzz all the time—oh," she said, her expression wise now. "That's the problem, isn't it? You and Buzz. Ever since that hayride. I thought you were in love with him. I thought he liked you, too."

"He acted like a . . . I guess they're all like that."

"What?"

"You know how boys are."

"No," Caroline said coolly. "How are they?"

"Look, I'm not talking about your brother or Teddy Roscoe. Maybe they're different. But most guys are only after one thing, and you know it."

"A good time," Caroline said, making a face, sarcastic. "Come on. Ted and I have a great time, and he never . . . ."

"Ted's different," I said. "He's just—well, he's so nice. I mean, you guys really have a good time together."

"Well, he is a great tennis player," said Caroline, laughing. "Which doesn't mean he keeps entirely to himself when we go to the movies. Exactly what did Buzz do to you?"

I sighed. "It was so wonderful at first, I mean, we were laughing and joking on the hayride, and then we danced, but then Buzz started kissing me and ... and ...."

"What?" Caroline breathed, watching me, rapt. "What'd he do?"

"He held me so ... close. Oh, Caroline, he touched me, I mean, he really started to touch me. All over."

"What'd you do?"

"I socked him."

"What? You socked Buzz Duarte? My God."

"In the stomach," I said miserably. "I didn't know what to do!"

"Well, if he was going too far, why didn't you just tell him to stop? Did you ever tell him? Did you say no?"

"No! I don't know why I didn't. I just ... just panicked. I was, he was ... oh, Caroline, I never felt that way before."

"What do you mean? What way?"

"When he was kissing me I—I felt ...."

"Oh."

"Do you know what I mean?"

"Sure."

"With Ted Roscoe? When he's kissing you?"

Caroline blushed a deep color. "I guess so. I mean, sometimes I don't want him to stop."

"Did he ever ...."

"Ted's pretty reserved." Caroline sighed. "I guess that's good. I mean, I don't have to worry. You can tell Buzz is—would be more, well, you know how he is."

"Yes."

"How'd he kiss?"

"Great!"

We laughed.

"I mean, did he French?"

I moved closer to Caroline, lowered my voice. There is nothing we haven't shared, ever since fourth grade when we met.

"Yes. He did."

"Did you like it?"

"No. Yes. Oh, shoot." I giggled.

"How did you know how?"

"I . . . ." I sighed. "Caroline, some things you just know. I just opened my mouth a little ways, and he, he put the tip of his tongue in it, I mean, not in it, but he touched the tip of my tongue and we . . . ." I opened my mouth to show her, then burst out laughing, and Caroline giggled too, and soon tears were rolling down our cheeks. I sat back finally and sighed again. "Oh, Caroline, it was the most wonderful feeling! Do you think sex is like that? I mean, when you really do it?"

"I'm sure it is."

"How do you know?"

"My mom told me."

"You talk to your mom about things like that?"

"Oh, my mom loves to talk about sex. It's probably her favorite subject. I tease her about it."

"Are you girls studying in there?" my mother called out.

"Sure!" Caroline and I chorused, and we began to giggle again, holding our hands over our mouths.

"We probably ought to start our reports," I said.

"What are you going to write about?"

"Mrs. Ebert said we should write about something we lost. But I never lost anything. Nothing important. Nothing I'd want to write about."

"She just wants us to start telling her things about our feelings." Caroline rolled her eyes. "She's a real nut. Thinks she's a shrink or something."

"Well, have you got any idea?"

"Yeah!" Caroline cried, jumping up gleefully. "Let's write about how you lost your virginity at the hayride!"

"Not funny. Look, if we don't get started . . . . why don't you write about that time you lost your tooth? When you fell off the bar in fourth grade?"

Caroline looked thoughtful. "Yes. I could. But what's the big deal? Everyone loses teeth."

"But that wasn't a baby tooth," I reminded her. "And it's how we got to be friends." Caroline had just moved out here from Wisconsin. I saw her fall, and I took her to the girls' bathroom and got her a wet paper towel to sop up the blood. She was shaking and crying so hard, not just because of the tooth, I realized, but because she didn't know anybody. That day I went to her house and met her folks. They were so different from my parents. Her mother talks all the time, about everything. She laughs a lot. Her dad does research in desert biology. He's quiet and wears a dress shirt even in the house, and fusses over his stamp collection. He's about opposite from my father, and Caroline's house is that way too, with paintings and books all over the place, and classical music on the stereo.

"Make an outline," I suggested. "Like Mrs. Ebert said." I went for my binder, but found no clean paper left. "Did you bring any paper?"

"No." Caroline laughed. "I didn't think we'd really work."

"I'll go get some."

My father usually had a thick pad of paper on his desk. Ordinarily I would have asked him first if I could borrow it, but something prevented me. Maybe it was Caroline. It seemed babyish to have to ask permission. We walked to the end of the hall and opened the door to my father's den.

We were not actually forbidden to enter his room. When we were little, Becca and I were not allowed to open the closet door because that was where Daddy kept his pistol. Somehow, the taboo against the closet had extended itself to the entire room, so that entering it we always felt a sense of awe. This time, with Caroline just behind me, it was no different.

I looked on top of the desk. No paper. I saw only his beautiful portfolio of maroon leather edged in gold, in which he kept his flight charts and instructions. I pulled open the center drawer. No paper. I said, "I'll go ask him."

"Maybe in the closet," Caroline said, pointing.

"Maybe." There were shelves in the closet; probably Caroline was right. I opened the door and smelled the rich cedar wood.

"Are those your father's uniforms?" Caroline asked.

"Yes." I realized we were whispering. With effort, I lifted off one of the hangers. Proudly I displayed the navy blue uniform with the shining buttons, the gold braid and the small embroidered emblem on the pocket.

"That's gorgeous," Caroline crooned appreciatively.

"Sometimes we get to fly with him," I whispered.

"I know."

We stood silent for a moment; my thoughts were slow, almost reverent. Twice my father had taken Becca and me to Phoenix, once to Hawaii, many times to San Francisco—free, of course.

"You're so lucky," Caroline murmured.

I had stepped into the closet. A low bookcase inside the closet was filled with leather-bound notebooks, magazines, and several cartons, but none contained paper.

"Let's go," I said.

"What about that?" Caroline pointed to a large blue canvas flight bag.

"Wouldn't be any paper in there. I think that's where he keeps his matchbooks."

"Why does he need so many matchbooks?"

"He collects them," I said proudly, "from all over the world." I pointed to some on the shelf in a huge brandy snifter and others in a heavy glass box.

"He must have millions of them if that bag is full," Caroline said.

I shrugged and, curious, lifted the bag. It felt heavy, pulling to one side, as though a living creature waited there, asking to be let out. I pulled at the zipper.

"What is it? Is it matches?"

"No. Letters."

I reached into the bag, pulled one out, and the breath caught in my throat as I read the return address. Alissa James. 1732 De Bois Street. San Francisco. Why, I knew her!

Suddenly my mother's voice piped out, thin and high. "What are you girls doing in there with your father's things?"

I turned, dumbfounded, slipping the letter into the pocket of my jeans, while Caroline, stammering, began to back away.

"Nothing, nothing," I gasped. "Looking for paper."

"I guess it's time for me to go home," said Caroline.

"We weren't doing anything wrong," I said quickly.

Mother put out the light and shut the door, holding the knob for an extended moment, as if to keep whatever was in there sealed forever. Later, I wished she had.

4

THE LETTER in my pocket had to wait. Becca came bouncing in to show me her diorama, so far only a carpeted box with the tiny glass unicorn in it.

"Lovely," I said. "Now leave me alone. I've got homework."

"Will you read my report when I'm done, Inky? Please."

"Sure," I said. "Where'd you get all your information about unicorns?"

"From the encyclopedia," she retorted. "That proves they're real."

"Oh," I said. "Have you ever looked up dinosaurs? Or witches?"

"What's that got to do with it?"

"Forget it. Hey, Becca, do you remember Alissa James?"

"Who?"

"Don't you remember that time in San Francisco, when Daddy bought you your unicorn, and I got the dragon?"

"Sure. But who's Alissa?"

"Never mind." I was aware of the letter in my pocket; it seemed to radiate its own heat.

I waited until ten o'clock, which is usually quiet time in our house, and lights out. Nobody checks or anything, it's just routine. While I waited I read my social studies chapter, but with only half a mind. The other half was on that visit to San Francisco nearly two years ago.

Alissa James was the lady we met at the coffee shop. It had been a magical day, ending with a show and going out for cake that was seven layers high, filled with lemony nut filling and topped with a frosting so delicious I can taste it still.

Daddy and Becca and I were standing at the counter almost ready to leave. Behind the counter on shelves lining the entire back wall was the most gorgeous display of stuffed animals any of us had ever seen. We stood staring, Becca and I, unwilling to ask, for the trip to San Francisco, the museum, and the movie were already fabulous treats—not to mention the exquisite little cake shop. Neither Becca nor I would have had the nerve to ask for more. But our father must have seen the desire on our faces. He said, "How about one each?"

We gasped and stared at him, pretending not to understand. "One each? One of *what*?"

"A gift," he said. "One for each. You have exactly three minutes to make your choices."

We giggled. Becca could spend hours deciding, deliberating, asking everyone's opinion. Of course, we all knew exactly what she would choose: The unicorn.

It was white and fleecy, with brilliant blue eyes, a golden horn, and sweet little hooves of black felt. The mane was long and silken; the nostrils flared as if the little beast had been running. It was the most beautiful and perfect little unicorn, about twelve inches long. Becca took it into her arms; and since then, it has always stood in the place of honor on her headboard, guarding her sleep each night.

I chose a dragon, long and green, with diamond shaped fins and a wide mouth to breathe out smoke and flame. I keep the dragon on my bureau, its tail curled around the frame of my mirror.

The two years seemed like a mere shadow when I saw that name, Alissa James. It all came back in a rush, how we stood there as Daddy paid for our presents. We clutched them happily and prepared to leave for the airport. It was about seven in the evening and we would be home late. It had been one of those odd schedules for Dad, a last minute substitution for another pilot who went home sick. That was why we got to go along. He had a six-hour layover in the city.

We were almost at the door, my father putting away his change, looking down at his wallet, when we heard the swish of movement, then light laughter, and all at once an astonishing array of bright colors and sounds overwhelmed me.

"Peter!" came the woman's voice, filled with laughter and happy surprise. "What a coincidence to see you here in town!"

My father's face froze with astonishment. Then he laughed, flushed, grasped me and Becca by the shoulders and pulled us to him, at the same time holding us a little away, as if we were prizes to be admired.

"Alissa! It was an unexpected trip. Last minute. These are my girls. This is Becca. And this is Inky. Girls, this is Mrs. James. Mrs. James is . . . ."

She smiled, showing beautiful white teeth and a lovely, soft mouth, brightly painted.

"Your father and I are old friends," she said. "He has told me so much about both of you! Inky, I am delighted to meet you at last. Rebecca! What a beautiful unicorn."

The pronunciation she gave to my name, that trace of something slightly foreign, made it sound romantic, like those unusual names that belong to beautiful, mysterious women. Like Alissa herself.

She wore a purple silk dress, so plain, yet so stunning. It danced around her legs when she moved. It caught the light in some spots, like water marks painted onto the fabric. The light from the ceiling of the little cake shop caught in her black hair, making it shine. She was colors and brilliance. Laughter showed in the corners of her lips and in her eyes. It fluttered in the movements of her hands and in the little tossing motion of her head.

We stayed only a few minutes. We had to leave for the airport. On the way my father told us that Alissa owned an expensive boutique on Post Street, where he often went to buy things for Mother. Mother's present last Christmas, in fact, had come from Alissa's shop. She was a friendly and clever woman, and, my father looked meaningfully at me when he said this last, a lover of fine things, especially art.

So Alissa and I had this in common. Perhaps that explained why I was so instantly drawn to her. But I felt guilty for liking another woman, comparing her to Mother. They were nothing alike.

Now, with the house silent, I picked up the letter. I took the paper from its envelope. It was cream colored stationery edged in blue—feminine, elegant, and with the letters "AJ" embossed in the corner.

"Dear Peter!"

I had never before seen anyone close a salutation with an exclamation point. It seemed charming and exciting. I read on, expecting to find something about her shop. But that was not what was there. I glanced at the green dragon on my bureau, reminder of that night. It seemed to leer at me as I read:

Dear Peter!
You can imagine how surprised I was to bump into
you the other night. My heart was pounding so terribly
that I was afraid everyone would know instantly.
Peter, your beautiful, beautiful girls! So fresh! So
innocent! But of course, any children of yours would
be beautiful, my love.

I felt as if something had gotten a hold around my
throat, some reptile. Still, I read on.

Loving you as I do, I don't see how I can go for another
month without seeing you. Then I realize it doesn't
matter as long as I know there will be those golden
moments for the two of us. We are entitled to that, I
think, after all the years of duty and dry, dead
relationships. How ironic it is, my love, that you live
so near the desert, and how symbolic!

Exclamation points danced across the page, just as her
purple dress had danced around her legs. I saw Alissa
differently now. Loathing was like a taste in my mouth,
like raw liver I had once eaten, on a dare. Hatred overwhelmed me, not only for Alissa, but for him, too. My
father.

I waited until it was very late. I could hear the baby
owls hooting outside in the trees. Then I crept out into
the hall and to my father's den, at first to replace Alissa's

letter. But as soon as I stood there with the closet door open and the bag unzipped, its contents beckoned to me like forbidden jewels. I felt completely calm, though my heart pounded; I have never felt that way before. I sat down on the carpet and read other letters from Alissa. One mentioned the maroon leather portfolio.

I searched high and low for exactly the right gift, Darling! Happy birthday, my beloved.

I dug deeper. There were other letters with other postmarks, other names. There were snapshots. My father with a very pretty young woman wearing a red jumpsuit. My father with a snorkel, flanked by two laughing ladies in bathing suits, holding his arms. I'd never known he had gone snorkeling.

I heard the hiss of my breath, like air rushing from a tire when it has been slashed. Now I understood why we kept a box at the post office, why no one but Daddy had the key. He brought our mail whenever he came home after flight duty. All the time I had thought it was only because he delighted in bringing us the mail and distributing it all around.

I took all the photographs and letters I could hold and stole back into my bedroom and stuffed them under my mattress.

In the morning, when Grandma came to wake me, I must have looked sick.

"But what is it, child?" asked Grandma gently. "Are you unwell?" It is her term for the monthly period. Mother calls it the curse.

"Yes," I said shortly. "I am unwell."

She urged me to stay home in bed that day. Part of me wanted to. But I couldn't do that. I didn't want to be at home. I went off to school as usual.

5

I KEPT the letters and photographs under my mattress. For the next two nights, when the house was silent, I put on my lamp and took them out to read again. It was like a wound, a scab you pick until it opens up again and bleeds.

Alissa's final letter was postmarked six months ago. She had written her farewell. The most recent letter, postmarked only a month ago, was from a woman named Gail in Mexico.

Dearest Peter,
What a fabulous weekend. I must admit I was worn out for four days afterward, but who's complaining? Of course I want to see you if you can get the Puerto

Vallarta route. I meant what I said! Well, gotta go, sweetie. Much love,

Gail

At school I just followed the usual routine, numb. Caroline was busy preparing for a tennis match so I couldn't talk to her about my discovery. I couldn't tell Barbara or Krista; we just were not that close. So I kept it to myself, but I couldn't stop thinking about it: my father, those letters. At home I avoided him. I went out on my bike or stayed in my room supposedly doing homework. He was leaving again on Friday and for the first time, I was glad.

For him, everything was as usual. He was king of the world. "Hey, Inky–Dinky, I'm leaving tomorrow," he said. "Let's have a game of Fra–ha."

"No thanks," I said coldly. "And please call me Ingrid, or at least don't call me Inky–Dinky. It's a stupid name."

He made his monkey-clown face and moaned, in comic exaggeration, "Don't ya love me just a little?"

My mother's face was bland, and she murmured, "Inky, be still. Here. You can shell these peas." She set the bowl down with a bang.

"Well, Becca will play, won't you, sweetheart," my father said. And soon I heard them outside, laughing and playing as I sat at the kitchen table, miserably shelling peas. My mother can always find something boring for me to do.

I looked at her now as she stood at the stove, browning meat for stew. Her hair coiled itself into the tight little waves that no amount of brushing or washing would ever unkink. Mine would have been the same, except that I straightened it. I like sleek, straight hair, like Caroline's.

I looked at my mother's pale skin. She never wore makeup, only lipstick, which quickly faded. Her brows and eyes were pale, washed-out looking. She wore old gray cotton pants, with many bulging pockets, and her terry cloth scuffs. I couldn't help thinking of Alissa James, how beautiful she was.

The front door slammed as Becca and my father returned. Minutes later I heard the shower and his voice raised in song above it. He always bellowed out the same song, "Home, home on the range, where the deer and the antelope play." He seemed not to know the rest of the words, for from there he would go, "Da-da-deedle-de-dum-dum-de-dum!" I used to watch him standing at the wash basin shaving, with only a towel tied around his waist. Now the thought of it made my face sting.

I brought the pan of shelled peas over to the stove. My mother had not seen me approach, and she scolded, "Inky, why do you always come sneaking up on people? Good heavens, it's enough to make a person faint."

"I'm sorry." An idea came to me with a rush. "Mom, is Daddy going to be gone all weekend?"

"Yes. He's going out tomorrow."

"Well then, maybe you and I could go to Castle on Saturday. If you don't want to drive," I said hastily, "we could take the bus. I thought we could go shopping. Maybe you could have your hair done. You know, like that picture you got last week from *Woman's House*. Remember how you said you loved that haircut? You could even get a tint. Mom, you'd look so great! We'd have a super time."

"Forget it, Inky. You know I hate going to Castle alone."

"Not alone!" I cried. "I'd go with you. You could have your hair done, maybe even your nails, and you could buy some new clothes. Maybe a dress. Something pretty."

"Inky, stop pestering me. I've decided to put up some marmalade on Saturday. It wouldn't hurt you to help."

I was near tears. It was no use. I could never persuade Mom to go to Castle and get herself fixed up. Never.

"Listen, Inky." She drew me aside, took my hands into hers. "I don't mean to be cross. It's just that my back has been bothering me. Sometimes it hurts me just to walk. I know you'd like me to be more—well, like other mothers. I'm sorry. Can't you understand?"

"Sure," I said.

At dinner Becca talked about school. Her friend Tina was going out for the soccer team.

Mother frowned. "I've heard that people get kicked in the mouth playing soccer," she said.

"They wear face guards," said my father. "The goalees."

"Well, just the same," said my mother with a sniff. "It's up to Rebecca, but I wouldn't be caught dead on a soccer team."

"Marguerite," said my father, "you don't know a damn thing about soccer."

"What's next for you, son?" asked Grandma. She sounded anxious, as if each trip would be his last.

"Puerto Vallarta," he said. "A new route."

Gail, I thought.

"That's nice," Grandma said.

"This meat is tough," said my mother. "Peter, do you think I should get my money back? I don't know. Maybe it wasn't the butcher's fault."

"Sweet Marguerite," crooned my father. "Never gets mad."

Mother flushed slightly. "Well, I don't like to be unkind."

I watched my father's face as he continued eating, unconcerned. He seemed like a stranger: handsome, tan, with strong lines across his face, from smiling. My father, I thought, and a cold feeling washed over me. A liar. A cheat.

Grandma chattered brightly. "Midge Greenley's granddaughter was elected homecoming queen at her college. You remember her, don't you, Marguerite?"

"I sure do," said my mother with a sniff. "They live way up on the old Mason Road. I wouldn't drive up there again for anything. Last time we went, four years ago, she didn't even offer us a cup of tea."

"Well, well," said Grandma. "I guess she was real busy."

"I figure, if she's too busy to offer me a cup of tea after I've taken the trouble to go all the way to her house, she's not the kind of friend I need."

"Well, well," said Grandma, and with a faint smile she turned to me. "You'll be homecoming queen yourself someday, Ingrid. I know you will. You're such a pretty girl."

I sat there biting my lip. Ordinarily I would merely have laughed. I am not the least bit pretty. My lower lip is too large. My hair is just brownish blond, and my eyes are pale blue. Like mother's. Becca is the pretty one. She has Dad's glossy dark hair and dark eyes. She is small and soft looking, with a beautiful smile.

"Who cares?" I said. My tone was sharper than I'd intended. "All that homecoming business is a bunch of hype." I felt enraged, ready to burst out crying.

Grandma brushed her fingers distractedly over the tabletop, whisking off crumbs. Then she said, "Peter dear, would you please pass the stew?" Her hand shook as she took the platter.

Becca stared at me. Rotten me.

I got up. "Excuse me, please. I've got a report to do. I need to go to Caroline's. She has some references."

"You know we don't like for you to go out on school nights," Mom said blandly.

"This is important," I said, gasping. "It's urgent. Caroline has a book I need."

"Let her go," my father said. Somehow he must have known I was ready to blow a fuse.

"How will you get there?" my mother asked.

"I'll ride my bike. Please! It's perfectly safe. Please, I'll be home by nine."

"Go ahead," said my father.

"Thanks, Daddy."

I turned to see him grinning, and he gave me a wink. Pals, the wink said. Confederates.

Caroline lives only eight blocks from me. I got there in a few minutes. Her folks were still at the supper table, talking. From the stereo came delicate sounds. Caroline's mom answered the door.

"Inky!" Mrs. Faust welcomed me. "You're just in time for dessert. Caroline is out in the kitchen getting it." She laughed. "Pudding cake, her specialty. That's why I can never lose any weight."

"That's not the reason," said Mr. Faust. "She bakes, you eat. One has nothing to do with the other."

Mrs. Faust crinkled her nose, laughing, and gave her husband a playful swat.

"That'll cost you," he said soberly. He was nearly bald and humorless. But Mrs. Faust kidded him as if he were the greatest.

"Old fogey!"

"They're fighting again," said Caroline calmly, entering with a tray. "Hi, Ink. What do you think?"

It was her usual greeting.

"Chocolate? My favorite," I said, and sat down to join them. The pudding cake was delicious. Better, even, was the atmosphere. Calm. Nobody angry inside. I wondered, were they always this way? Or were the Fausts only putting on an act for company? The music was wonderful. I said so.

"Mozart," said Mrs. Faust. "Our favorite."

"Do you like him?" asked Mr. Faust.

"It's beautiful," I said. "We don't have any records like that."

"Oh? What kind of music do your parents like?" asked Caroline's mom.

"None," I shot back, before I could think how awful that sounded. But it's true. My folks never listen to music. I thought for the first time about how different I was from them. I love music, all kinds.

After the dessert was done, Mrs. Faust brought in small cups of strong coffee, and she and her husband settled back in their chairs. He began to talk about a magazine article he was writing, and he filled his pipe right there in the dining room. My father is only allowed to smoke in his den.

Later, in Caroline's room, I sat on the small loveseat her mother had upholstered for her, and I tried to figure out how to begin. I felt as though it were written on my face, that sense of betrayal and grief. Caroline didn't notice.

"Have you started your composition yet?" she asked.

"No. I've been too busy."

"Hey, my mom got this fabulous new nail polish. It's called Cinnamon Apple. Want to do our nails?"

"Would she let us use it?"

"Sure. Why not? You know she always shares."

I nodded, my throat tightening. Caroline didn't realize how lucky she was.

Caroline ran out, returning moments later with her mother's nail kit. "I asked," she said. "Just to make sure. Let's do our toes, too. Want to?" Caroline pulled off her shoes. I did the same, and we wadded little balls of cotton between our toes and began filing our nails with the emery boards.

"I guess your mom spends a lot of time on her nails and hair and makeup," I began.

"I don't know." Caroline bent over her foot, engrossed in painting her big toe.

"She always looks great," I said.

"Yeah? Yeah, I guess she does. Of course, she could stand to lose five or ten pounds."

"Men don't like women too skinny."

"My dad sure doesn't," Caroline said. "He doesn't want my mom to lose any weight. He just kids her about it. They don't really fight."

"I know," I said wistfully. "I've seen them at the market. They both push the cart."

Caroline laughed, handed me the nail polish. "Here. Your turn. My folks have known each other since college," she said.

"So have mine, but . . . ." The words, unexpressed, seemed to rattle and beat against my chest from the inside. Tell her, tell her, I thought, and then the beating inside would stop. "Your folks," I said softly, "seem like they were made for each other."

Caroline nodded. Her face became very serious, so that her skin looked almost transparent. Caroline is so beautiful, with soft creamy skin and that sleek smooth hair the color of amber. She wears it cut short, like a halo, and it never gets mussed. "Maybe that's because they've been through so much," she said. "When they were first married, my dad got very sick, you know. He was in the hospital and almost died."

"I didn't know that!"

"Yeah. And then they lost a baby. I would have had another brother. He died when he was only two weeks old. Crib death, they call it. I guess it made them close. I mean, they feel so lucky to be together now."

"I guess when things like that happen, people are . . . I mean, they appreciate things. They won't let anything spoil it. My parents never had anything like that. My mom's always talking about her back, you know, and not feeling well. But she never went to the hospital. And my father's always feeling great. Maybe that's why he . . . ." I looked at Caroline. "He needs other friends," I said.

"My dad doesn't have any men friends," Caroline said. "He does everything with my mom."

"My father's friends are . . . he travels so much that he meets people, and some of them are . . . ."

The word choked in my throat.

Caroline held out her foot. "Nice," she murmured, "but a little dark. Don't you think?"

"You never really know about your parents," I said, my voice thick. "You don't stop and think that they are really separate people. You know what I mean? They have their own lives. Maybe they do things we don't even know about."

"Well, of course they do," Caroline said. "So what? We do things they don't know about. I mean, did you tell your parents about Buzz? How you socked him? How you were making out and everything?"

"Well, there was nothing wrong with what I did!" I cried.

"Who said there was? I just said you didn't have to tell them. It's not like when we were little and we had to run to our folks all the time. I mean, we're nearly in high school."

"I wish I could go away to boarding school," I said. "I wish I could leave home. Except for Becca."

"I wouldn't want to leave," Caroline said. "College is soon enough. Why would you want to leave your mom now?"

I shook my head, realizing that I could not say anything to Caroline about my father and his loves. I glanced at the clock. "I've got to go, Caroline."

She walked me to the door. I called goodbye to her parents. They had moved into the living room, where her mom sat on the floor working on a photograph album, while her father read the paper aloud.

At home I found my mother sitting in the kitchen, embroidering. She embroiders pillow cases for all of us, and little guest towels for gifts.

"Hi. Where's Dad?"

"Watching some violent war movie on TV," Mother said. She continued stitching, humming quietly to herself. In the soft light her skin looked delicate and lovely, and her pale brows were like those in paintings I've seen of madonnas.

She is not like the other mothers, I thought, with a sense of shock, some shame, and tenderness. Caroline's mother gives piano lessons. Krista's mom loves politics, and Barbara's mother works for an attorney.

"Mother!" I called out. The intrusion made her prick her finger, and I saw a bright drop of blood bubble up on her flesh. She sucked it away with a slight shudder.

"Why do you do that?" I asked.

"What on earth are you talking about?"

"Embroidery. Why do you?"

"What a silly question. What else would you have me do?"

"You could join a club. Help out at the library. Do volunteer work at the hospital. What would you like to do?"

"I would like to be able to sit here and embroider, without anybody bothering me with questions. Or is this a riddle?" She threaded her needle again. "When you were seven, you were always asking me riddles. Do you remember?"

"I wish I was seven again."

"I wish I were fourteen."

"I have a riddle for you," I said, and something seemed to grow in me, like a thorn, something mean. "Why would a person marry a pilot? It's like being a sailor's wife. I would hate being alone so much. Why does he always travel on weekends? Doesn't he want to be home with us?"

All this came bursting out of me. Oddly, mother did not seem to notice. She only shook her head, then bent to do a tidy French knot and murmured, "When you're a little older, Ingrid, you will understand these things."

She sewed for a few moments longer, swift, brisk stitches. Then she surveyed the partial picture held tight in her little embroidery hoop and nodded with satisfaction.

"Did you finish your report?" she asked.

"I can't even get started," I said. "It's such a dumb assignment. Something we lost—I never lost anything. How can I write about it?"

Mother put her embroidery down. "But Inky," she said, "there are all kinds of losses. What about Roger? Can't you write about him?"

My face must have registered horror, for the next moment Mother rushed to me, smoothing back my hair and saying, "Inky, I'm so sorry. Had you forgotten? Oh, how unkind of me to say that. I'm sorry."

"It's all right," I murmured. Now the recollection was sharp and complete of Roger, my tortoise: his crushed shell, the underbelly bleeding and filled with pus, the leg ripped off and that gaping hole—I had loved that tortoise so much that after the death I cried for two days. How could I have forgotten?

I went into my room, sat down at the desk, and wrote five-and-a-half pages about Roger. I wrote about how I had found him one morning under the magnolia in our patio, and how, four years later, I lost him forever. It still hurt.

6

I WAS ABSOLUTELY mortified. Mrs. Ebert read my composition aloud in class. She must have rehearsed it, because when she was finished a few of the girls were actually crying.

Across the aisle, I saw Buzz Duarte leaning way forward in his seat, listening.

Mrs. Ebert gave her little speech, about reaching inward and sharing willingly one's experiences. Pain, she said, is always part of growth. "The author of this piece," she said, "has obviously been in touch with pain. And it has strengthened her. It has given her compassion, not only for the tortoise that she so dearly loved, but for all living things."

I sat there frozen. Maybe she wouldn't call my name.

Maybe she'd just pass out all the compositions and leave my private life alone.

But no. Mrs. Ebert held up the paper, as if it were a flag. "This was written by Ingrid Stevenson, class."

"All right, I knew it!" Buzz yelled out, half laughing, and other students made sounds of surprise, and I wanted to just dig a hole and crawl in.

"A fine piece," Mrs. Ebert said, handing me the paper. "Perhaps you have a potential career as an author," she added brightly.

I said nothing, just took the paper from her, too shaken to look at the grade until later, when we were out of school.

"A plus!" Caroline shrieked. "You got an A plus! Why the fuss? Here's the bus. You got an A plus!" Caroline sang out in her inevitable rhyme.

"Shut up and leave me alone, Caroline, can't you?" I snapped.

"Ink! What's wrong with you? What'd I do? I was happy for you, that's all. I never get A plus on anything."

Rotten me. I felt awful. "I'm sorry, Caroline," I said meekly. "I was just upset. About Buzz. He was laughing at me. I didn't think anyone could be so unkind."

"You think he was laughing at you? Why would he?"

"Let's forget it, Caroline. Want to do something?"

"I can't. I've got tennis."

"With Ted?"

She grinned. "You guessed it. We're getting ready for

the meet. Ted and I are going to be doubles partners."

"Have a good time," I said, heading for the bus. Once on, I couldn't find anywhere to sit except next to Betsy Carmichael, who is a nerd and a loudmouth. She's always fixing up people.

"I saw Buzz Duarte at the show with Judy Treehoff," Betsy informed me excitedly. She brushed out her hair, stroke after stroke.

I wanted to move or say, "Hey, don't brush your cooties on to me!" But, like a sap, I did nothing.

"So, you saw Buzz Duarte," I finally said. My voice was low, shaky.

"Oh, pardon me. Everybody knows you're crazy about him," said Betsy, flipping her hair. "How was the hayride?"

"Buzz means nothing to me," I said.

"Oh, sure. So I suppose you wouldn't care if I told you he's going to ask Judy Treehoff to go steady with him."

My heart pounded. Judy Treehoff. That tramp! I glanced around. I wanted Caroline. Why was I sitting here talking to a girl I couldn't stand? All because of Mrs. Ebert. Because I'd poured out all those feelings. Because I was scared and frantic and upset all the time. Why? Because of my father. What if Mom found out? They might get divorced. Who could I talk to? Nobody, nobody in the world.

Honestly, I don't know how it happened; but I started to cry. And I couldn't stop. Naturally, Betsy Carmichael misunderstood. She gave me her wide-eyed fish stare and said, "Well, you certainly do have it bad. I feel sorry for you." She kept brushing her hair, harder and harder. In a burst of rage, I grabbed the brush from her and broke it in half.

"What a creep!" Betsy screamed. "You broke my brush! You're going to have to pay for it. Oh, yes, you are." Betsy grabbed my purse. We had come to her stop, and I ran out of the bus after her, even though my stop is at least two miles farther on. I wanted to fight her, and as I chased after Betsy, I screamed, "Just you wait, I'll kill you! I'll break more than your stupid hairbrush!"

Scared, she threw my purse into the gutter, then stopped long enough to stare at me and say, "You are crazy, Ingrid Stevenson. You'd better go home before somebody locks you up."

I rescued my purse, then walked home. It was a long way, and with every step I thought about what I should do. *He lies to us. All the time. He cheats on us. On Mom. He sits here talking to us, but all the time he's thinking about someone else. Making plans. Going to hotels. With women.*

I could accuse him outright. I played with ideas, fantasized a sober, gentle, sensible confrontation, his embarrassment, and finally, his confession. He was sorry; he'd just been so lonely away from home all those nights. He loved us! Maybe he ought to take a different job, stay home more, have a real family life, like other fathers. The thoughts soothed me until I walked into my house and realized I could never, never say a word to my father about it.

The house was oddly silent.

"Becca!" I called.

No answer. On her headboard stood the little unicorn, its gold horn thrusting upward.

I lay down on Becca's bed, her pillow under my stomach, and stared up at the unicorn, whispering to myself, doesn't he love us? How can he do it? Who is with him now, lying in his arms?

"Mother!" I called.

No answer.

I ran through the rooms. Then I remembered. They were all going to the supermarket to buy pumpkins for Halloween. I'd said I wasn't interested, thinking I'd be with Caroline. Now, I stood there in the empty kitchen with a mounting sense of panic, like the panic I'd felt at the tryouts, everything spinning, my lips numb and tingling, my mouth going dry.

I ran into my father's den and flung open the closet door. I grabbed the travel bag with its letters and rushed out of the room, then out the front door.

On my bicycle, I fled.

PAST DRYER'S MORTUARY and the Lucky Seven Motel, along the two-lane boulevard and then onto the tar road I pedaled, my legs pumping swiftly, without tiring. I was possessed of some new energy. The road dipped and lifted; gravel sprinkled the edges; small smears of sand crunched under my tires until I reached Lankersheim's Dairy and smelled the cows. I saw the broken barns whiz past the periphery of my vision.

Seven Wells, I thought. Seven Wells. I chewed over the idea that my town's name was in error. I had looked all over and found only three old wells in all. Seven Wells, why did they name it that? I searched for wells out of the corners of my eyes as I sped along, as if by solving that mystery I would be free. My father's flight bag flapped against my side, a heavy weight that I would soon discard. I'd show him!

I rode out into the desert, hearing echoes of my mom's voice. "I wouldn't be caught dead out in the desert alone!"

I didn't care. I wanted to be alone.

A dead lizard lay in the road. I let my wheel run over it, imagined the ooze of its guts; I didn't care.

A car rushed past. I felt the wind and the vibration, and my bicycle wavered, yet I continued. It was hot. I could smell the sagebrush, an oily, sharp oder. I saw a mound, then the decaying skeleton of a small mouse over which a long, thick line of ants crawled. They had eaten out the eyes and only holes remained.

I had not noticed until then how ugly the world was.

Screeching to a stop, I skidded and scraped my knee on the road. I didn't care. It didn't even hurt.

I set down the flight bag, unzipped it and pulled out a great handful of letters and photographs. Engrossed, I ripped them into little bits, and then I let them go.

The desert breeze blew the scraps all around me. I reached for the remaining few. One was the photograph of my father with his snorkel. This I put into my shirt pocket, along with the first letter I'd found, from Alissa James. The rest I ripped into tiny bits and tossed them aloft. Finally, I swung the flight bag around and around, like a discus thrower, turning myself faster and faster until the desert was one hot blur. I released the bag, watched it sail away and land at some distance near three cacti, caught in the prickles.

"Whatcha doing, girlie?"

The voice boomed at me.

"You doing some kinda voodoo?" Laughter followed, harsh and cackling, the sound of an old man.

I recalled how my mother would say with a shudder, "Look at that old desert rat," meaning not rats, of course, but vagrants. "Poor soul," she'd murmur, but she'd swiftly roll up the car window.

The old man had come up behind me. Shirtless, he wore overalls, the straps of which lay against his withered, dark flesh like a harness. The folds of his elbows, throat and face resembled the hide of a hippo, the skin tanned and thick from years of sunlight. His teeth were bronze colored, crooked and rotten, so that his smile was a horror. I must have turned pale.

"Doncha let me scare you. I didn't mean ta scare you. Just going to my place." I could smell his breath, stale from beer.

"Your place?" I looked around, stalling, holding myself firm against fear. There was nobody else around. Nobody but the desert rat and me. "What place?"

"It's sorta camouflaged, you might say." He pointed, and I could smell his body's sweat and other strong odors of neglect. "Over there behind those boulders by that little scrawny tree. My place. Wanna see it?"

"No, no. I haven't time. I—I'm meeting someone."

"Like in the army, we used to camouflage stuff, you know? Dug into the hills, slept and ate and played cards down in those trenches. Know what I mean? Naw, you weren't even alive then, little girlie like you, I mean the big one. You know?"

I nodded. "The war," I said. "The big one." The man carried a stout stick in one hand and a net bag in the other. The bag was nearly empty, containing only a paper carton with a McDonald's label and a bottle of Gatorade. Obviously, the carton could not have contained food.

"Bugs," said the man, as if in answer to a question. "I have a collection. Best place for 'em, the desert. You come to my place and see 'em if you want."

He stepped toward me, his hand outstretched, and I saw his weakness, yet I also caught an expression in his eyes that made me grab my bicycle and pedal away as fast as I could.

Behind me I heard a shout, "Hey, girlie! I'm not gonna hurt you!" I did not look back, but followed the road to the crossing, then took a sharp left, then another, then a right, riding on and on until I realized I was lost.

To be lost in a crowd is one thing. To be lost in the desert on a dirt road is something else. I stood there, squinting out to the low hills, hearing a strange beating like a distant construction site where heavy hammers pound, but the pounding was in *me*. My heartbeat.

"I wouldn't be caught dead out alone in the desert." The words rang back to me again and again.

I gazed at the telephone poles; they crisscrossed the landscape. Soon it would be dark. I sat down at the edge of the road, my heart still pounding, forcing myself to think.

Bits of advice came back to me. "If you're ever lost, stay on the road. Don't wander. Don't panic. Something will come to you."

Whoever said that?

My father.

Something will come to you.

I don't know how long I sat there. Time seemed to stretch. I saw the shadow, then the shape of a large bird. Looking up, a sense of calm replaced my terror. There, boldly etched against the sky, just ahead and to the left, I saw what I first thought was a mirage, and instantly realized was a beautiful hot air balloon. With a surge of hope I rode toward it.

7

I HAD NEVER SEEN a hot air balloon before, except in photographs. This one seemed to have sprouted, new, this very hour out of the desert, a vivid red, blue, and yellow. It looked like a painting.

As I neared the site, I saw that the balloon was tethered to a tall, stout pole, and that some hundred yards behind it stood a clapboard house, weathered and sagging. The large front porch was littered with cartons and a couple of old metal chairs.

As I approached, a dog appeared, barking happily. It was black with large white spots on its face and a white patch on its chest. Its ears were wavy, like a spaniel's, and they flapped up and down in an excited dance.

"Hi!" I bent down, and the dog licked my face. I've always wanted a dog.

"Annie, what in tarnation are you barking at?" came a woman's voice from the house, firm and stout, the kind of voice one hears in the country. "Prob'ly got herself a lizard, silly thing. Quit that noise, or I'll tie you to the rafters!"

The door slammed. Out came the woman, wearing not a country quilted dress and apron, but blue jeans and a man's short sleeve shirt, with the sleeves cut down and the collar removed. She was not stout, but robust, her figure firm and tall, and her hair piled high into a knot atop her head.

"Why, hello there," she called, reaching for the dog, which immediately threw itself down on its back, begging for a tummy rub. The woman bent, stroked the dog's stomach, smiling up at me all the while. "Gus!" she called into the house, without turning her head. "We've got company. Our first guest. Gus, come on out here. And bring something to drink. She looks thirsty."

The woman's face was dusted with freckles, and her hair was streaked blond and pale brown. Her eyes were very blue, Irish blue, and there was a natural rosy tinge to her cheeks and a brightness in her face that I immediately liked.

She extended her hand to me. I gave her a quick smile and a handshake.

"I'm Mary McMurphy," she said. At the slam of the screen door she added, "This is my son, Gus. You brought some lemonade? Good. Have a glass, dear. You must have been riding for hours. You look all flushed. What's your name?"

"Ingrid. Ingrid Stevenson," I said. I noticed that her fingers were stained with paint, and a cloth hung out of her back pocket. "I'd love some lemonade. I didn't know anyone lived out here."

Mary McMurphy and her son both laughed as if I'd said something marvelously funny. They led me to chairs on the porch, and Mrs. McMurphy sat in one, I in the other. Gus leaned against the porch railing, drinking lemonade, looking at me with laughter in his eyes.

"We're laughing," said Mrs. McMurphy, "because the place is so dilapidated it's no wonder you haven't seen anyone. We're just fixing it up. Painting." She showed me her hands. "I see green in my sleep."

"I like to paint," I said, then blushed.

"Want a job?"

I smiled, embarrassed; I'd been too eager, I knew.

"You must have seen our balloon," Gus said proudly. "Didn't I tell you, Mom? It's the best advertisement."

"I did see it," I said, relaxing a little at last. I drank until the glass was empty, and Gus refilled it from the plastic pitcher. I wondered, did she mean it about a job? I'd love to stay here and paint. Something out here was peaceful, clear.

"Have you been here long?" I asked. I figured Gus was about seventeen or eighteen. Much too old for me, of course. Of course.

They laughed again. "Two days," said Mrs. Mc-
Murphy. "And Gus had to get that balloon up first thing.
We're not open for business until next week, but Gus
figured this was the best way to let people know we're
here. We just arrived from Tucson." Mrs. McMurphy
nodded toward the old truck that stood in the drive, a
large black Ford that bore scars of long service.

"Drove out here with everything," Gus said, "including the balloon. We've got two baskets for it, all the
equipment. You a balloonist?"

Now it was my turn to laugh. "No. I've never even
thought of it."

"You'll think of it now," Gus said, smiling. Gus was
tall, and his jeans were too short, as if he'd grown a
whole lot in the last few months. I could imagine Mrs.
McMurphy laughing and half-scolding, saying, "My
land, it's only been four weeks, and you've outgrown
your pants again!" Then I could imagine the two of
them climbing into the truck and roaring down to San
Diego to buy new jeans and sneakers. Maybe staying
over to see the Wild Animal Park, eating tacos and
drinking Cokes and then, unwilling to end it, going for
a late night walk in the zoo to chat with the baboons and
the hippos. That is exactly what I would do if I could,
that is, if anyone at my house were anything like Mrs.
McMurphy with those freckles and that terrific, ready
smile.

She threw up her hands suddenly and ran into the
house, bellowing, "Oh, Lordie, the soup's burning! Why

can I never make a pot of soup without burning it at the bottom? Darn! I'll have to scrape it out."

Gus laughed and called out, "Never mind, Mom. I wouldn't know it was homemade if it didn't have a touch of carbon in it." He winked at me and added softly, "She's really a great cook. But I don't praise her too much. I want her to keep trying."

I wondered again—did she mean it about a job? I didn't know how to ask.

"Where do you live?" Gus asked.

"Seven Wells."

"Oh, yes. I think we drove past there. But that's quite a ways," he said, frowning for the first time. "About seven or eight miles, isn't it?"

"I'm used to riding far," I said.

He pointed. "I guess you rode straight down that road," he said. "As I remember, you come in at the old church just outside of town."

I realized then that I had ridden in a great arc, and that if I followed the road Gus indicated, it would take me straight to the church, which was about half a mile from my house. A long ride, but certainly possible to do. I glanced up at the sky. The sun was dipping down toward the horizon.

"I should be going," I said.

"Why don't you let me drive you?" He moved toward the house. "I'll just get my keys. We can put your bike in the truck. It's getting onto sunset and . . . ."

"No!" My tone was too sharp, and I quickly covered up by saying, "I'm not allowed to take rides from anybody."

"Well, all right," he said, dropping back to the porch railing again. "Did you mean it about painting? We could sure use the help. I hate doing the trim."

"I like painting with enamel," I said.

"Then you'll come back? Maybe tomorrow? We've got the whole interior to do."

"I'll try to get back," I said. "If I can." I didn't know what I'd be doing the next day. My mother might find something for me to do, as usual. At that moment I realized I didn't want her to know about Gus. I had found an oasis. Sometimes you get a certain feeling about people right away, and somehow I knew my mother would spoil it if she knew. "I wouldn't be caught dead out there with those types," she'd say. "Balloonists?" she'd sniff. "It's really up to you, Inky, but I've heard they are a rowdy bunch." Suddenly I saw it: My mother doesn't really like people much. She doesn't have any friends.

"A week from Sunday," Gus went on, "we're taking our first flight. Maybe your folks would like to go up. We've got room for four in the basket. We're going to have a coupon in the local papers, so it'll only cost twenty-five bucks apiece. It's a promotion," he explained. "Usually it's sixty bucks."

"We couldn't," I said, moving off the porch now and toward my bike. This was true. No way in the world would I ever get my mother into a balloon, she who wouldn't even drive to Castle, who got "funny flashes" in a crowded department store, and who never went to movies, saying she preferred to sit in her own living room watching television.

"Couldn't?" Gus gave the word a queer ring, as if it wasn't even in his vocabulary. "How come?"

"Well, you see, it's just my father and me," I said quickly. "My mother's dead."

I was amazed at myself. I knew it was a weird thing to say. I hadn't planned it, the words just popped out. And once said, they were permanent.

"So I have lots of chores to do," I went on. "I have to take care of my little sister and—and everything. I just came out here to . . . to think."

"Oh, I am sorry," Gus said, looking embarrassed. "Well, anytime you want, you can come and watch."

"Thanks," I said. The way Gus looked at me, I felt suddenly older. More responsible. As if it really was just Daddy and me, and I was in charge of things.

"Thanks for the lemonade," I added, and casually, "See you around."

"Anytime," he said.

I got onto my bike, then looked back at him. "Ingrid," he called after me.

"Yes?"

"I think you would like riding in a balloon." Gus waved and smiled.

He should only know. A balloon? I got dizzy just from standing on a chair. Looking at him there, I knew

he'd never understand, but just laugh at me. Gus Mc-
Murphy was the kind of person who wasn't afraid of
anything.

I rode off, my right hand uplifted in a farewell, trying
to look casual. I rode fast, and my skin tingled as the
wind brushed against it. It was dusk. The desert lay in
shades of lavender and blue. The sky was crimson, shot
through with golden streaks, turning to purple. I thought
how beautiful it is out in the desert in the evening, and
I felt sorry for my mother who never went out to enjoy it.

It was dark when at last I reached my house, ex-
hausted. The first star hung above the house, and I gazed
up at it and made a wish. It was a wish without words,
but its effect was a single idea. Gus.

As soon as I opened the door, my mother screamed,
"Where on earth have you been?" Then she began to
cry. "I've been frantic, sick with fear. How could you
do this to me? If you knew how worried I was. Don't
you care about anyone? Oh, God, I thought you'd been
kidnapped."

"Then why didn't you call the police?"

"Well, your bike was gone so I knew . . . ."

I had caught her in a lie, and I was about to lash out.
Then I realized that I was the biggest liar of all.

"When your father gets home," she said, angry now,
"I'm going to tell him. Don't think I won't. Until then,
you're grounded. Do you hear me? Home right after
school. No bike rides, no *nothing*."

8

✳

MY MOTHER had never grounded me before. Her
anger and the punishment made it seem that we were
all changed. The house itself seemed to stiffen. Becca
cleaned out all her dresser drawers. Even Grandma was
subdued and stayed in her room all that Saturday morning. By noon Mother had taken to her bed and called
Dr. Henry. Her back was "acting up again."

Dr. Henry came. He is mild and very soft spoken, and
he always smells newly washed. He looks small and
fragile, and a straw colored moustache shades his mouth.

He smiled his sad little smile at me and said I looked
"peaked." "Maybe a slight touch of anemia?" he suggested, and wrote out a prescription for iron tablets.
"Common in girls your age," he added, patting my arm.

For Dr. Henry, everything is "slight" case. My father

always imitates him, until we are doubled over laughing, Becca and Grandma and I. Mother's lips twitch at my father's parody, though she scolds, "It's downright unkind to make fun of people, Peter. Dr. Henry is a fine man, and he still makes house calls."

"Well, well, a slight touch of leprosy," my father will continue, sending us into peals of laughter. "I believe you will soon experience a slight dropping off of fingers and toes.

"What an old-fashioned old geezer!" my father says. We have to laugh; it is true.

My mother defends him. "It's a rare doctor who doesn't practice in the city, chasing after the almighty dollar!"

"You have a good word for everybody," my father croons. "Sweet Marguerite. What a renegade I am by comparison!" He grins. "But don't ya love me just a little?"

Dr. Henry examined Mother, pressing gently on her back. "Here? Does that hurt?"

Mother only nodded, smiling bravely. "A little."

"Well, backs are no picnic," said Dr. Henry, a statement that I filed away for later use; my father would eat it up. "But you're bearing up, my dear. How are those pills I gave you last time?"

"They do upset my stomach, Willard. But I hate to complain."

"Now, now." Dr. Henry patted her shoulder. "We should try something a little milder. And stay off your

feet, my dear. You do altogether too much. Is that marmalade I smell? Do you mean to tell me you put up your
own preserves?"

"Well, just a few jars," she said shyly. "Won't you
try some? We have fresh bread."

Dr. Henry, Grandma, and Mother made a party of
it. Mother served tea from her little flowered pot. Becca
and I each took a hunk of bread and jam and left; Mother's look indicated that I, being grounded, was not included.

Being grounded on the weekend is terrible. And of
course there was no way I could get out to the Mc-
Murphy's. They'd think I wasn't interested. They'd find
somebody else to paint the trim. I laid on my bed, moody,
trying to sketch.

Becca threw herself on my bed.

I yelled, "Get out of here, Becca! Why can't you ever
leave me alone?"

"I thought you'd like to play."

"What do you think I want to play? Crazy eights? I
hate crazy eights."

It was a low blow. Becca adores card games.

"I'll play anything you want," Becca said.

"Let's play mummies," I said.

"How do you play that?"

"We wrap a gauze bandage around your mouth and
make you lie absolutely still and leave me alone," I
snapped.

Becca laughed. "Oh, Inky, you're so funny."

I didn't feel funny.

Becca ran to get the big box that contained her life-time accumulation of paper dolls and accessories, pictures of houses, dishes, trees, furniture, which we had through the years clipped out of magazines.

"Let's play paper people," Becca murmured, already transported into that other world.

"No," I said, but my tone was feeble. I protested only for show. It was irresistable. We loved playing paper people, creating new worlds.

"You can choose first," Becca said, laying out all the paper people, handsome men, lovely women, slick looking teenagers, little children, and even babies.

I chose a strikingly handsome teenage boy with a deep cleft in his chin and bright blue eyes. He was dressed in a bathing suit; his clothes had been carefully placed in an envelope and labeled. Becca was very orderly.

"All right," Becca said, choosing a girl. "I'll be his sister."

"No. You should be his girlfriend."

"If she's his sister, they can do everything together. He won't have to go home in the evening."

"He still won't," I said. "He can stay at her house."

"He cannot!" Becca objected.

"Look, Becca, he can. They're just paper dolls. They can do anything they want. They can even . . . ." I stopped. I wanted to talk about it, what they could do. I felt suddenly wicked and wild, worse than Judy Treehoff, whom everybody talked about because of the things she did with boys.

Becca was bent over the box, selecting dresses, humming softly to herself. Innocent Becca, I thought, appraising her body, the flat chest and plump arms, the round, child's face.

She put a sweatsuit onto her doll. "Let's take them jogging."

"He doesn't have a jogging suit," I grumbled.

"He can wear shorts and a T-shirt," Becca said. "They're going jogging and then out for hamburgers. He's going to ask her to go steady. He's really in love with her. Maybe they should be about twenty, and then they can get married, Inky, and we can use the bridal clothes from the other doll and . . . ." something suddenly changed in Becca's tone.

"What's wrong, Becca?"

"I think Tina's parents are splitting up."

I didn't know what to say. Becca and Tina do everything together. I could see that Becca was scared.

"That's awful," I said. "What happened?"

"Nothing. They just fight all the time, Tina said. Her mom went away alone last month. When she came back, they decided to split. Tina says it's too late. They won't change their minds."

"Why won't they?"

Becca shrugged. "Her mom said if her dad wouldn't go to a marriage counselor, she'd leave him. Her dad wouldn't go. What do the counselors do?"

I frowned. "I guess it's like a counselor at school. Probably they help you. Give you ideas. About getting along better."

I could tell Becca was ready to cry. She gets this certain look on her face. She covered up by rummaging through the paper doll things, chattering too fast. "They should have pets. I'll give my girl a pet unicorn." She dug through the box and brought out a picture of a unicorn with a chain of flowers around its neck. "There," she murmured to the paper doll. "This is your pet unicorn, and he'll protect you always. Unicorns are strong. They're faithful. We'll name him Pierre. That's French for Peter."

"No!" I cried, grabbing Becca's hand. "Becca, you know very well there's no such thing as a unicorn. It's a myth. Nothing but a story. You've got to grow up. You act like a baby. Look at Tina. Her parents are splitting, and she's going to have to learn to—to adjust," I said, as I visualized poor Becca trying to put her life together if our parents should ever separate. She was such a baby! How could she make it?

Becca got that look on her face. Then she said fiercely, "Just because you never saw a unicorn doesn't mean unicorns don't exist. You never saw an earthquake either. You've never seen New York City."

"It's common knowledge, that's all," I retorted. "Listen, you believed in Santa Claus until you were seven. I never did. I knew from the time I was four it couldn't be possible, but you . . . you . . . ." I reached for the unicorn.

Becca cried out, "Inky, don't!"

Too late. We heard the rip. The paper unicorn was torn in half, and Becca, stricken, began to cry.

"Shut up! Shut up, you baby!" I yelled, afraid Mother would come in, and I'd be in trouble again. "Quit that crying, it's only paper, you baby, we can tape it."

But Becca ground her teeth and grabbed my arm, using all her strength, trying to hurt me, twisting the skin for an Indian burn. "What do you know about unicorns? Nothing! Nothing! Daddy told me he even saw one, down in Argentina one time; and if you think he's lying, you're really horrible."

"He's lying," I said looking at her straight on.

"Inky, you're horrible. I hate you. I hate you so much!"

"I hate you, too," I said, and I meant it. "I wish I could leave this house forever. I really do."

I'M NOT SURE who ended it first. But somehow that evening Becca was in my room again, and we'd spread out all the paper people on my bed. I had my stereo on low playing an old Beatles song. Becca loves music.

"Maybe her dad will change his mind," Becca said. "Maybe he'll go to a counselor."

"I hope so," I said, not needing to ask whom she meant.

"Tina says her father never wanted any children."

"Doesn't he love her?"

"I don't know. He always watches TV with her. They play badminton sometimes."

"Lets dress our dolls for bed," I said, yawning. "I'm tired."

"If he didn't want her, how come he got her anyway?" Becca asked.

I was startled. Didn't she know? "Becca," I said, watching how her hair fell over her face, how she concentrated on her little paper doll and laid the paper clothes gently away. "Becca, what do you know about babies? I mean, where they come from."

"I know everything," she said.

"Everything? Who told you?"

Becca shrugged and flung her long dark hair back from her face. "Oh, you know. Mom told me some of it. And the kids at school. And Daddy."

"Daddy? Daddy told you?" No. He wouldn't. Mom had only told me about the monthly period. Nearly everything I knew had come from Caroline, except for those lectures we got at school. How could Daddy have spoken to Becca about such things? And why had he never spoken to me?

I tried to remain calm. "What did he say? When? Why didn't you tell me?"

Becca shook her head, laughing. "What's the big deal? He just told me that babies are born from seeds. The way flowers and trees and vegetables are planted."

"Seeds!" I burst out. "You mean, like you buy them in a packet at the hardware store? Like that?"

"Inky," she cried, exasperated. "You know very well what seeds he meant. They're in people. In the man. Put into the woman. Why are you asking me? Don't you know? Daddy told me everything I need to know. Someday I'll get married and have babies, like Mom had us, and it will be so exciting. It will be wonderful. We can all live close together, you too, with your husband and your babies, and we'll all have dinner at each other's houses, and picnics on Sundays . . . ."

I looked at my little sister, and I wanted to give her a hug. Instead I said, "Hey, let's go have some hot chocolate."

She leaped up, beaming. "Oh, yes. Inky, you make the best hot chocolate in the world."

"Let's get into our pajamas first. The way we always do."

"Can we have marshmallows in it?"

"Sure," I said. "What's hot chocolate without marshmallows in it?"

9

MY FATHER had been gone for five days. Puerto Vallarta. Gail.

Mother met him at the door. I was in the living room watching TV. Between our living room and the hall is a wooden divider of lattice work. I could see my parents through the diamond-shaped slats.

"Mail call!" my father shouted. "Everybody out, time for presents."

Grandma came shuffling out, holding out her hand. "Did my check come? My social security check?"

"It sure did, Mama. And an advertisement for dancing lessons. How about it? Shall we take the course together?"

Grandma laughed and nodded. Daddy was in fine form.

"Inky! Becca! Where are the girls?"

I saw my mother stiffen, then heard a bitter burst of words. "...impossible. I grounded her...how frantic I was! Flat on my back for three days. You've got to do something."

"Poor Marguerite," my father said. "Look what I've brought you! Inky, come here at once."

I turned off the TV, expecting to see him angry. But he wasn't. His face was tanned, and he looked exuberant. "I'll talk to you later, young lady," he said, but I read the twinkle in his eyes. It said, we'll put on a good show. For her. We'll settle this between us.

He held out a small white box. "For you, princess. Did you miss me?"

I didn't know what to say. All those nights I'd been thinking, wondering, worrying, and here he was, as if nothing had happened, quite as if nothing was wrong at all. Well, as far as he knew, I realized, everything was the same as always.

I took the box. In a way I hoped it would be something awful. I lifted the little cotton square and saw a pair of absolutely beautiful gold and coral earrings, for pierced ears.

"Daddy!" I breathed. I wanted to hate his gift, thinking of who might have been with him when he picked it out, hanging on his arm maybe, saying my name. But the sight of those earrings won me over completely.

"You like them, princess?"

"Oh, they're gorgeous. Thank you, Daddy. Of course,

now I'll have to have my ears pierced."

"Of course," he said, beaming.

It had been a matter of some discussion for months. Now Mother came to look. "Very nice," she said. "Do you intend to go through with it, then?" she asked, meaning the piercing.

"Yes," I said. I glanced at my father, and he nodded slightly.

"It's perfectly appropriate, Marguerite. They're her ears, after all."

My mother sighed and gazed down at her hands. "What does it matter what I think? Who ever cares what I have to say?"

"Where's Becca? In her room? I'll go find her," my father said. A while later I heard the shower running, and his bellowing voice singing out, "Home, home on the range!"

At supper my mother was wearing a new pin, a red rose made of enamel with thin golden coils for stem and leaves. Her cheeks, too, were red, as though she had dabbed on spots of pink blush. Now she served up the meat and macaroni and passed the plates around.

"As long as we have been married," my mother always told people, "whenever Peter comes home from a flight he has a little present for me. Without fail. It's like Christmas when he comes home. And he brings little gifts for the girls, too."

He never brought a gift for his mother. Receiving presents made Grandma cross. Nobody could understand or explain it; so whenever Daddy came home he just gave Grandma a kiss and squatted down beside her, as if he were a little boy again, and he let her look at him and ask questions. "Are you tired, my son? How was the food? Did it rain during the flight? Really, you must take good care of yourself, Peter."

"I will, Mama," he would say, his smile half tender, half teasing, like a little boy again. "I thought I'd take you dancing tonight, but since you want me to rest... well, I guess you don't really care. You've probably been out swinging with old Hank Potter while I was gone."

"Oh, Peter, go on, you're a bad boy to tease your mother that way." But she laughed and laughed.

"What shall we do tonight after dinner?" Mother asked, her smile suggesting glorious, exciting possibilities.

"We could play Clue," said Becca.

Grandmother looked up from her food, her eyes bright. "Oh, yes," she said. "Let's."

"Clue again?" Daddy laughed. "Well, if you all insist."

"I don't feel like playing," I said.

They all stared at me.

"Everybody plays," said my mother, her mouth tight. "It is a family game. Family night. Everyone plays."

"What if I won't?"

"Please play with us, Inky," said Grandma. She pushed a piece of macaroni around on her plate.

I gazed from one to the other of them. My father,

freshly shaved and showered, looked like a movie star in his crisp white sports shirt. Grandmother with her smile, seeking peace; my mother's face, flushed and flustered, with the red rose pinned to her gardening coat. How could they not know? Or were they just pretending?

"I don't want to play!" I screamed.

"Ingrid." My father spoke my name quietly, but with infinite authority. He got up, stood beside my chair. "Come with me," he said.

My hysteria and my objections swiftly faded; his face was a mystery. Trembling, I followed him. He led me outside to the vacant lot, to the enormous oak tree with its trunk so large you can't get your arms around it. From here we could see faint twinkling lights far in the distance, shooting through the haze that always hangs at the edge of the horizon. Usually the view and the breeze from here made me feel terrific—but not this evening. My only sensation was a pain in the pit of my stomach.

My father put his arm around me.

I stiffened, my shoulder signaling, *let go!*

He dropped his arm, turned and lit a cigarette. He smoked in silence for a few moments, exhaling long streams of smoke, and then he said, "What's going on with you?"

"Nothing."

"You go out without telling your mother. You come home after dark. Where do you go?"

"Out."

"On your bike?"

"Yes."

"Do you meet other kids?"

"Sometimes."

He took another deep puff, then ground the cigarette out under his shoe. "I see," he said. Then he asked, "Are you in any trouble?"

"No."

"Then what are you hiding? Why won't you tell us when you go out?"

"Freedom!" I shouted. "I need to be free!"

I had not thought the words, but they came ringing out, a desperate, urgent cry.

He turned away from me. I saw his profile as he gazed out toward the distant lights. Then softly he said, "I can understand that, Ingrid. Really, I can. But you must realize that your mother worries about you."

"She shouldn't worry so much," I cried.

"Sometimes it's hard for people to change."

"She grounded me for four whole days."

He began to walk slowly, around the tree, down the slope along the path that led, ultimately, to the village. "Mothers always worry," he said. "Look at Grandma. She still worries about me, and I'm forty years old."

"But you still do what you want," I said, breathing heavily. The words were at the edge of my mind—now, now I could say it, tell him the truth. Now, if ever.

"Nobody can do everything they want," he said soberly. Then his voice changed, a light tone. "I take it you are interested in some boy? It would be odd if you weren't. A pretty girl, a girl your age ... your mother has spoken to you, I know. You're a bright girl. You know how to handle yourself with boys. Am I right?"

"Oh, Daddy." My face burned with embarrassment, with unspoken accusations. I could never, never confront him. *He's my father.*

"So, look, you can go out in the afternoon, and if something comes up, a group of kids going out, or a boy wants to take you to the show or a dance, you can go. But you have to check with your mother and me first. Is that understood? And you have to be home at a reasonable time. Fair?"

"Fair," I murmured.

He gave my shoulders a squeeze, then quickly let go, as if he remembered some new signal. Don't touch.

We had walked several blocks from the house, and now as we turned he said, "Becca's very upset about Tina's folks. Did you know that? It might help if you take her in tow a little. You know. Play with her after school. She wants to go out for soccer. Lord knows, she needs the exercise."

"I will," I said. And then, "Tina's father won't go to a marriage counselor."

"Becca told me all about it." He laughed, swinging his arms as he walked, his old self again, jovial. "I guess Tina's parents would just die if they knew their kid had blabbed their personal story all over town."

"Well, why won't he go?"

"Who knows, princess?"

"Would you? That is, if Mom asked you to?"

"Look, princess, you know I do anything your mother wants. All I want to do is to make her happy."

"But if she wasn't happy, if she wanted you to go, would you really?"

"Yes, yes, really. Hey, some of my best buddies have gone in for counseling. Come on now, let's go in and play Clue." He made a funny face. "I know your Grandma can hardly wait."

FOR THE FIRST TIME in a week I fell asleep right away, feeling somehow safe again. I don't know how long I slept, but at the edge of wakefulness I heard angry voices.

Then it started.

I had heard them fighting before, it seemed like a thousand times. My father's voice begins with short, sharp thrusts. It expands, increases, louder and louder, until you feel things shaking, the walls, the beams, and you want to bury yourself deep, deep, but nothing can mute the terrible sound of his anger.

"I told you never to take my things, didn't I? I can't trust you for a day, for a minute. Stealing my things, going behind my back when I'm away trying to support this family, doing my best, working eighteen hours a day without a rest. What do I get for it?"

"I never took anything. Peter! Maybe it was Mama." My mother's voice was a pathetic wail.

"Then you must lock her in her room. If she's too

senile to leave things where they are, what's to prevent her from burning the whole house down? From going into the streets naked? Do I have to get a padlock for my door?"

My mother's gasping wail was worse than the thundering shout, worse, worse, and I lay shrunken into a ball, tight, under my covers.

No matter what she said, no matter how soft or pleading or sorrowful her tone, he would go on until he was spent; there was nothing to do but to let it all out, that fury that shook the house and turned my blood to ice.

"What possessed you?" he screamed. "I tell you, it is lack of respect for my property, for me. It is your way of spitting on me, of showing your utter contempt. I won't allow it, I tell you. I am the man in this house. I won't allow you to step on me, to make a fool of me." He would be shaking his fist, shaking something he had grasped as a weapon, a shoe or stick or cooking implement; once he had taken up a knife. He never struck. But the threat was always there.

"I didn't touch it. I didn't take it," Mother whimpered. "Maybe it was stolen. I told you, the door was left open the day Inky ran out...I told you I would never take your things."

"What were you thinking of, what were you looking for? Spying on me, always the spy. Liar! Liar!"

I pulled the blankets over my head, pulled my knees up to my chest, tight. Still I could hear everything.

"I didn't, I swear it, Peter. Oh, Peter, I swear it to you."

"Enough. Be still. I can't bear that sobbing. Enough!"

It was hard to believe that this was the same man who had spoken to me out by the oak tree just a little while ago. He was like two different people. One to play and joke with, a jolly clown, the other like a mythical thunder god, who with a single blow can strike you dead.

10

THE NEXT DAY after school I rode out to Gus's. This time, taking the direct route, I saw that the place had a name: Shea Station. My mother assumed I was going to Caroline's, or over to the mall. I guess my dad explained to her that I needed some freedom. We agreed I'd be home by six.

"What's doing!" Gus greeted me with a big smile, responding to Annie's excited barking. His shirt and hair were splotched with paint.

"Annie's got a green beard!" I called.

"That's why she has to stay out today," Gus said. "If you've never seen a dog put her nose into a paint bucket, you haven't lived. She was totally green. I saved all the trim for you," he added.

"Thanks, I think." I laughed. "I couldn't get back sooner." I paused. The lie about my mother had been haunting me. Maybe now was the time to correct it.

But Gus waved aside my explanation. "Look, I know you have other things to do. Actually, I've no right to get you to do my work. Except," he laughed, "it's just so much fun. I mean, maybe you should pay me for the privilege."

"It won't work," I told him, grinning. "I read *Tom Sawyer*, too."

"You don't have to paint," Gus told me, as I followed him inside to the huge living room, piled with boxes and rolled up carpets. "You can just keep me company."

"Oh, no. Let me help."

Gus got me an old shirt and a cap that said "Morro's Gardens."

"What's that from?"

He reddened. "Oh, a place I used to go to a lot in Tucson."

"Did they give hats to everybody?"

"Well, I knew the owner real well."

I knew right away there was some connection with a girl. I could tell by the look on his face, the way he turned aside and busied himself shaking up the paint. "You like to do enamel, you say?"

"I'll do the mantle." It was a large, carved mantle now painted an ugly brown. In pale green it would be beautiful.

I began, carefully dipping the brush, pausing to let the color settle, then firmly applying paint with a long stroke, evening out the brush marks with the tip.

"Looks like you're really experienced," Gus said admiringly.

"Well, I've done this before. I painted my own room and the bathroom last year. It took me over a week."

"What color?"

"Blue. My favorite. I was going to do a mural on the wall by my bed. Somehow I got busy."

"You're an artist, then?"

"Well, I'm not great. I've just always done drawings. Ever since I was really little."

"Maybe you could make a poster for us."

A clacking noise in the background suddenly stopped, and Mrs. McMurphy came in. "Ingrid! How nice to see you. Gus, did you offer her any refreshments first? Or did you just enslave her immediately."

"The latter," Gus said.

"Oh. Very nice. How about a Coke?"

"Sure."

"We've got a cooler out on the porch," Mrs. McMurphy said. "It'll be great for the customers." She laughed. "And for us, too. Gus and I are real soda pop freaks."

"We all have our vices," Gus said.

"How true," said his mother, momentarily solemn, then laughing again as she pulled the clip from the top of her head and let her hair settle around her shoulders. "Ingrid, if you know anyone who needs typing done, tell them I'm interested. Reasonable rates, good work."

"Oh, that's the sound I heard."

"So far, no customers. I was working on our promotion."

"Ingrid said she'll make us a poster," Gus said. "She paints."

"Oh! An artist. That would be fabulous, Ingrid." She came to look at the mantle, turning her head in surprise. "No wonder you do such beautiful work. Gus, take a look. This is really professional."

"One Coke, coming up," Gus said, letting the door slam behind him.

"I'm glad you came," Mrs. McMurphy said, smiling. "Gus was getting lonesome."

"Hey, Josh!" We heard Gus calling from outside, and Mrs. McMurphy and I looked from the window to see the mail jeep coming by, and Gus running toward it. He returned in a moment, bounding up the steps with the mail. Swiftly he glanced through it, pausing over a letter written on the kind of stationery only a girl would use, with a seal on the back. This he put back into his pocket and gave the rest to his mom. A look passed between mother and son; I felt like an intruder and reacted to the first thing that met my gaze. It was a large wooden chest, intricately carved with dragons and Chinese symbols.

"What a beautiful box," I exclaimed, thinking of my dragon at home.

"Don't open it," Gus warned.

"Why not?"

"It's full of old receipts and photographs," said his mom, laughing. "We call it Pandora's box."

"Who's Pandora?"

"From the Greek myth," Mrs. McMurphy said, "Pandora was a young girl who was given a box and told never to open it. Of course, curiosity got the better of her. She opened the box."

"And got a lot of old bills to pay!" quipped Gus, handing me a cold Coke.

"What really happened?" I asked.

"All the world's troubles came flying out," said Mrs. McMurphy. "At least, that's the story. I'd better get back to work."

The clacking of the typewriter accompanied us, almost like a song in the background. Gus and I didn't talk much as we painted, he the large wall, I the mantel and the door frame. I kept thinking of Pandora's box. And somehow I knew Gus was thinking about the girl who had written him the letter. I wondered who she was and what she was like, whether he loved her. He probably had lots of girlfriends.

Suddenly I asked him, "Gus, how old do you think I am?"

He stopped working to look at me quizzically. "Oh, I

don't know. Fifteen, maybe? Sixteen?"

"I'm fourteen," I said.

"Oh," he said. Then he grinned. "O.K. I was fourteen once myself. Only," he added, "I used to lie about my age."

"Why?"

"So I could do things I wasn't supposed to."

"Like what?"

"You don't really want to know."

"Yes I do."

"It would shock you. I'm sure you're a good little girl."

"Shock me. Let's see if you can."

"Well, I'd take the car out. I'd find a store that would sell me beer. I smoked. I fought quite a lot."

"You're right," I said, putting my brush into the turpentine to clean it.

"About what?"

"I shouldn't have asked."

"Now that you know all about my rowdy past, will you still come back?" He left his painting and squatted down beside me as I swirled the brush around in the can.

I looked up at him, meeting his eyes, dark brown eyes, very gentle.

"Of course I'll come back," I said, my voice a strange whisper. I straightened up. "After all, the trim's not done yet. I've still got to do the door."

"Mom will want to pay you," Gus began.

"No. Please."

He shrugged. "All right, Ingrid. We'll think of something. A reward."

It was enough reward, I thought, biking home, just to be there at Shea Station.

Coming home was like walking into a dismal cloud, especially when I heard my mother call. "Inky! Could you possibly get dinner started? I've been waiting for you all afternoon. My back's been acting up. And Grandma can't find her glasses. And would you call Tina's and tell Becca to come home?"

"Yes, yes," I said.

"You know how I depend on you, my dear," my mother added weakly.

I dreamed of Pandora's box that night. Only it was nailed to the floor of my father's closet, and when I opened it, a million insects flew out, each with a voice, each screeching, "Inky's a liar. Liar. Liar!" In the dream, along came my father. I felt his arms around me, strong, lifting me up. "All right, princess, it's over," he said, and lifted me into the box and closed the lid. As the lid came down, I vanished.

Gasping, I woke.

FRIDAY NIGHT was Halloween.

Becca was going out with Daddy. He loves Halloween. She was dressed up as Wonder Woman in dark blue leotards, a blue satin cape, mother's boots and some old silver bracelets that Grandma found in her trunk.

"Ready, princess?" My father, dressed in his uniform and a rubber ape mask that fully covered his head, gave his arm to Rebecca. "I'm ready to escort you, milady," he intoned.

Daddy always used to take me out when I was small. When I got tired, he'd carry me on his shoulders.

I went to my mother's room to tell her I was leaving. She lay on her bed, feet propped up on two cushions, reading a romance novel.

"I'm going over to Caroline's now," I said. "Remember, you said I could stay overnight."

"Just don't stay up talking all night."

"We won't."

I waited for my mother to ask what we were going to be for Halloween. She never did.

"Be sure and tell Grandma you're leaving," Mom said. "I don't want to have to go answer the door."

"I will." I went to her side, bent to give her a kiss on the cheek. "I love you," I said.

"What brought that on?" She seemed startled.

I shrugged. "When you were a kid," I said, "did you go out trick-or-treating on Halloween?"

She shook her head. "We lived on a farm, Inky. Things were different. There was always a lot to do. Besides, I'd have had to walk for miles to take in six houses."

I hesitated, then offered, "Do you want to go out with Caroline and me? Tonight?"

"Heavens no!" she exclaimed with a laugh. "I wouldn't be caught... thank you for inviting me, Inky.

It's sweet of you. But I'm best off here, relaxing. You go on and have fun. But be careful. Don't take any apples or things that aren't wrapped. And if you eat yourself sick, don't blame me."

"I won't."

Grandma was already in the hall, waiting for the trick-or-treaters. I kissed Grandma and hurried to Caroline's, on the way passing groups of little kids with their moms or dads, carrying flashlights, squealing and chattering with excitement.

At Caroline's, the old enthusiasm claimed us again; we laughed and loved every minute of the preparation. Mrs. Faust helped us paint our faces and fix our hair. We wore black tights, boots, and T-shirts, and we decorated our waists and wrists and necks with ropes and chains borrowed from various collections of hardware. We greased our hair until it stood straight up, applied purple and orange powder, and when we emerged from the bedroom to show Caroline's father, he actually screamed.

"What have you done?" he exclaimed. "Will it come out? How could you? Oh, I hate Halloween. Can't even read in peace, and now this."

"Relax, dear," Mrs. Faust said. "They'll be good as new after a shower. Quit worrying."

Caroline gave me a look as we went out to meet Krista and Barbara. "It's only hair. He's so square."

"Caroline, do rhymes come naturally to you?" I asked. "Or do you think about it."

"I don't know what you're talking about," she said crossly. "You know, my dad never took me out for Halloween. Never once. All he wants to do is sit there and read."

We hurried to Krista's house, and after admiring each other's costumes, we went trick-or-treating until our pillow cases were stuffed, and then we walked along Fallon Street where the high school kids hang out.

Suddenly a blast of music sounded and a truck appeared, with loud speakers, and dozens of helium balloons rising from the door handles.

"Hot air balloon rides!" boomed out a male voice from inside the truck. "Come to Shea Station, grand opening this weekend."

Gus, I thought, my heart pounding. Gus!

"Special this weekend, only twenty-five dollars, come one, come all. Hot air ballooning, a thrill a minute, the greatest trip on earth."

"Wow, twenty-five dollars," groaned my friends when the truck had rolled away. "Who can afford it?"

"It's usually sixty bucks," I said.

They were surprised. "How do you know?"

"ESP," I replied flippantly.

That night, late, Caroline and I lay in bed talking softly. I told her all about Gus, how I'd met him, how I'd gone back to paint.

"So," she asked solemnly, "are you in love with him?"

"I don't know," I whispered. "Maybe. I think he has a girlfriend back in Tucson."

"But he invited you over to paint."

"Maybe he just needed the help."

"Did he ask you out?"

"No. I told him I'm only fourteen. He probably thinks I'm a baby."

"But why did you have to tell him that?"

"I wanted to. I had to."

"You should have gone up to the truck and talked to him. He might have let us ride on it. It would have been neat."

"No! I couldn't. I didn't think he'd come to Seven Wells. I wanted it to be—I just wanted to see him at his place. You know."

"What are you talking about? Why can't he see you in Seven Wells? Are you ashamed of him? Don't you want us to meet him?"

"Caroline, I told him something. I—I lied. He thinks my mother is dead."

"But why would you tell him that?" Caroline sat up and snapped on the light.

The sudden wave of light hit me like a chill wind, and I began to shiver, braced against the cushions, my knees up to my chest.

"What's wrong, Ink? What is it?"

"Oh, Caroline. It's so awful. I've wrecked everything with Gus. My whole life is a mess. Remember the night you were at my house and we went looking for paper in my father's den? Well," I tried to keep my teeth from chattering and took a deep breath. Still, I shivered. "I found something else. Something really terrible. I mean, I don't know what to do."

"What is it?"

She came to sit on my bed.

"Promise you won't tell anyone."

"You know I won't. I can keep a secret."

Whispering, I told Caroline everything.

11

CAROLINE was wonderful. I mean, she really listened. At last she said, "What are you going to do?"

"I don't know," I said miserably. "I'm just scared. Maybe they'll get divorced. Anyhow, I don't feel the same about my dad. I guess I never will."

Caroline nodded. She asked, "Are you going to tell your mother?"

"I don't know. I keep thinking about it."

"Maybe you could get them back together again. You know. Closer."

"I've thought about that," I said, frowning. "But how?"

"Maybe if they went on a vacation together. Barbara's folks just got back from Hawaii. Barbara says now they're all starry-eyed. He kisses her in the kitchen while she's cooking."

"My parents never go away together. I don't think my mom's ever had a real vacation."

Caroline gave me a long look. "See? That's it."

IT WAS LIKE an omen when my father announced he was taking two weeks off from work. Usually he takes time off in the summer, when he can be with Becca and me. He usually takes us someplace. Mother always stays home with Grandma. Why? She says she hates the zoo, that boats are dangerous, long car rides make her irritable, hiking hurts her back.

Maybe they just hadn't found what they both liked, I thought. Hawaii would be perfect.

I told them that evening, making my voice casual, "You know, I could stay here and take care of Grandma and Becca if you two wanted to go on a vacation together."

My father looked surprised. "What? What made you think of that?"

"Why not?" Now I warmed up, and my voice was excited. "It would be romantic. Like a second honeymoon. I'll take care of Becca. I'll even clean the house. We've got plenty of food in the freezer—we could go shopping before you leave. If anything happens, I'd just call Dr. Henry."

"Sounds like you've got it all planned," my father said with a strange look of amusement.

"Well, I just thought—Barbara's parents just came back from Hawaii, and they . . . ."

"Since when do you make our plans for us?" Mom snapped.

"Marguerite, she's trying to be nice."

"Why do you want us to leave?" Mother demanded.

"Actually," said my father, "I was thinking of going down to Ensenada for a few days for a little deep sea fishing."

My mother looked up from her stitching. "Well, that sounds very nice, Peter."

"Maybe Mom would like to go!" I cried, my voice out of control now, nearly frantic. "Why don't you try fishing just for once, Mom? You might love it."

"I wouldn't be caught dead on a fishing boat, Ingrid. You know how I hate the smell of fish. If you catch any, Peter, please have them cleaned before you bring them home."

"Of course, my dear."

"Who are you going with, Daddy?" I burst out. "Can I go too? I could take off school for a few days. I'd love to fish!"

My father stretched and yawned. His tone was casual, almost lazy as he answered, "Actually, my friend Walter asked me to go."

Liar! I screamed inside. Liar! It was Gail he was going to be with, and I was outraged.

"Well, why can't I go along?" My head actually spun with anger.

"Because you have school, that's why," said my mother. "And because it's no place for you on a boat with two men. Now stop pestering, Inky. I mean it."

"You don't care if he goes away without us!" I screamed. "You don't even give a damn!"

"That's enough, young lady!" Mother rushed toward me and struck my cheek, hard. "Never let me hear you cursing in this house again, do you hear? Now go to your room."

I fled, hearing them behind me.

"What's gotten into her lately? So moody. So mad all the time. I hardly know . . . ."

"It's the age, I suppose. I dread the next four years, Peter, I really do. Adolescence. It's a curse. And then there's Becca next."

"Becca's an angel," my father said. "She always will be. We're lucky we only have one that's difficult."

"So you're back! What's doin'?" Gus greeted me as if he had expected me, like a regular visitor to the balloon launch.

"Not much." I had taken the early bus home, and without entering the house, had taken my bike from the garage. I hoped mom would assume I'd stayed at school for the game. My friends had urged me to stay and try out for Roadrunner, but I couldn't. I told Caroline, "I'm going over to Gus's. He's expecting me."

"What's he like, Inky?"

"He's so nice. He tells me things. And he listens. Not like Buzz Duarte. Do you realize, Buzz has never said more than a sentence or two to me in his entire life?

All we did that night was laugh at people's jokes and then . . . ."

"That's what I like about Ted," she said. "He isn't just always so physical."

"In a way I wish Gus would be physical," I said, and we laughed.

"Has he ever kissed you?"

"He hasn't even touched my hand."

Now Gus gave me a grin and a wave. "Almost done," he said, indicating the paint job. "I did my bedroom last night, and Mom did hers. All that's left is the kitchen."

"That means lots of enamel," I said. "You need an expert."

Mrs. McMurphy was already in the kitchen painting. "Hi! You're a life saver. My back is killing me."

"I know a good doctor," I said, then bit my tongue, hard.

Mrs. McMurphy laughed. "I have a better solution," she said. "I'll just sit down for a minute and drink an orange soda. Will you join me?"

Gus brought the sodas, and I drank mine as I began painting the cabinet.

"You really enjoy that, don't you," Mrs. McMurphy murmured.

"It's relaxing," I said.

"It must be hectic at your house," she said. "Gus told me you're in charge."

"Well no, not exactly. That is, my dad's gone a lot.

He's a pilot. So I have to take care of my little sister."

"How can you get away, then?"

"Oh, we have a lady come in to help some afternoons. It gives me some time off."

"And then what do you do for fun?"

I laughed. "I paint. Not just houses. I like to do water colors."

"Will you really make a poster for us? We could nail it to the shed, and maybe use the same design for our newspaper ad."

"I'd love to," I said. "I'll start tonight."

"Of course, we want to pay you," Mrs. McMurphy said quickly.

"Oh, no. I wouldn't know what to charge."

"How about a balloon ride?" Gus suggested.

"Perfect!" his mother exclaimed. "One free balloon ride. Payable upon request."

I said nothing, and the roar of a motor from outside saved me from reply. The mail jeep. Gus ran out.

"I'm glad when you visit," Mrs. McMurphy told me. "I need some female company once in a while."

I nodded. "I saw that advertising truck on Halloween," I said. "What a great idea."

"Gus thought of that. He's a promotional genius, I think. You should see how many people we had out here last Sunday. We had six balloons going up."

"Six? I thought you only had one."

"Ballooning is like that. Word gets around. Clubs come with all their members. They're always looking for a place like this—away from everything—where they'll be welcome. It's like a carnival, Ingrid. You'll love it."

Gus came running in, nearly knocking over the paint can.

"It came! My course. Boy, I've been waiting for this."

"That's great, Gus," his mother said. Her tone was sober, proud. Gus sat down in a chair by the potbellied stove and tore open a thick manilla envelope. He pored through the papers excitedly. I went back to my painting, and a few minutes later realized that Mrs. Mc-Murphy had slipped away, leaving Gus and me alone. A moment later I heard the sounds of her typing.

"She's got a lot of jobs already," Gus said. "Term papers, resumes, things like that. It'll help for her to be busy. When I leave, that is."

"You're leaving?" My breath seemed to catch in my throat.

"Oh, not for a while. But this," he indicated the folded papers, "is my ticket."

"What is it?"

"A correspondence course," Gus said. "I've only got three more courses to take, then I can enter college. Two of them will even give me advance standing at Pacific Grove."

"Pacific Grove!" I exclaimed. "That's a gorgeous place. But it's even farther away than San Diego. And isn't it terribly expensive?" I'd seen pictures of the campus, the low white buildings, palm trees, and vast lawns. It's halfway up the coast, along the beach.

Gus shook his head. "It's not all that bad. I've been saving for the last three years. By the time I finish these courses, I'll have enough for the first two years' tuition."

"Will you live there, too?"

Gus smiled. "Sure. I'll have to. Can you imagine me driving four hundred miles every day?" He glanced at the pages once more, then put them carefully away.

"What courses are you taking?"

He seemed to flush. "Oh, English and stuff. Prerequisites."

I felt like an ignoramus. "What are those?"

"Courses you need to get into college. Requirements. I never finished high school. But three months from now . . . ."

I bit my tongue to keep from asking more questions. I couldn't imagine someone not even finishing high school. And Gus seemed so *smart*.

"You know Josh? The guy that delivers the mail?"

I shook my head.

"He's a balloonist, too. He was out here last Sunday. A great guy. He'll help with the launching when I'm gone. He's working on his commercial license."

"Why do you want to go so far away to college?" The words just slipped out. I had no right to ask, no right to miss him, as I knew I would. Three months from now! It seemed too fast, too sudden.

"It's a great school," Gus said. "Besides, I need to get away. My mom and I have been . . . well, it's been just the two of us for three years now. We both need to be more independent. You know how that is. I mean, look, you're only fourteen, and you're already on your own most of the time. My mom thinks you're so mature."

The compliment took my breath away.

"I have to go," I said at last.

"Let me clean you up a bit first," Gus said.

He dipped a rag in turpentine and earnestly took my hands and cleaned them, doing it slowly, stroking each finger, the backs of my hands, the palms.

I stood motionless, gazing down at his bent head, flooded with feelings, both tenderness and shame. Mature, he'd said. Good girl, he'd said. Independent.

I imagined myself confessing: I've lied to you, Gus. My mom is very much alive, and my dad runs around with other women. My home life is a mess, and I've been a coward, afraid even to go try out for Roadrunner. Last week I got a cinch notice in algebra, and I hid it from my mother. My grades are slipping. I can't concentrate at school, and here you are, determined to make it all on your own.

I felt ashamed. Gus mistook my silence for something else. Very gently, he laid his fingertip to my cheek. It felt like a kiss.

12

MY FATHER had been gone for eight days. We settle into a different routine when he's away. There is less laughter, but also less tension. We eat simpler meals, and Becca and I fix ourselves late night snacks in the kitchen, whispering and laughing. When Daddy is home, he wants us in our rooms and quiet by ten.

"When's Daddy coming home, do you think?" Becca asked me. She seemed worried.

"I don't know," I replied. "I guess they must rent those fishing boats by the week."

"Why is he staying away so long?"

"They're probably having a great time," I said. "And his friend probably doesn't want to come home. He doesn't have a family, so I guess he gets very lonesome."

"So it's really nice of Daddy to be with him like that," Becca said, settling it for herself.

But I, too, counted the days, and I was worried. In school I couldn't pay attention to the teachers. Homework lay undone in my book bag, for the only thing I could really concentrate on was sketching. And Gus, of course. I attempted dozens of sketches of him. Even in class, my pencil seemed to move itself into those long, angular lines, the determined expression, the gentle eyes.

"Would you mind very much joining the rest of the human race, Ingrid Stevenson?" my algebra teacher rapped out in her sharp voice.

Laughter surrounded me. I caught Caroline's sympathetic glance.

"I—I'm sorry, Mrs. Murdock," I murmured.

"For somebody who has gotten a cinch notice," she continued, "I'd say your attitude is most peculiar." She strode over to my desk and picked up the paper. She stared at the sketch, at me, then put it down. "Apparently," she said, with the slightest trace of a smile, "your talents lie more in the arts than in math. However," she continued sternly, "that will not qualify you for college entrance, if that means anything to you."

It doesn't, I wanted to say. Instead, I only sat there, mortified.

Mrs. Ebert caught me, too. She found it "shocking" that I hadn't even started reading the assigned book.

After school, Caroline and I sat together on the bus.

It was our first time together since Halloween because she'd been staying late with Ted for tennis.

"What's new with you and Gus?" she asked.

"I'm going out there this afternoon to help finish the kitchen."

"And after that?"

"I don't know." I realized, after the painting was done, I'd have little excuse to go out there. It would look odd for me to keep visiting the McMurphys, especially if I didn't invite Gus to come to my house.

"They want me to go up in the balloon," I said.

"How super!" Caroline gasped. "Inky, think how fabulous, how exciting, how . . . ."

"You know how I am about heights," I interrupted.

"What do you mean? You mean you won't go?"

"Don't you remember that time we went skiing?" My dad had taken Becca, Tina, Caroline, and me to Mt. Baldy. I thought I could do it, but as the chair lift went higher and higher, I was gripped with panic. By the time we got to the station, I was paralyzed with fear. Two ski patrol guys had to pry me off the chair lift. I was never so embarrassed and so scared in my life.

"But a chair lift is different," Caroline said.

"Caroline, I get goose bumps just thinking about that balloon. I wouldn't be caught dead in a hot air balloon. Those things can blow up. Like that blimp that blew up, you know, the *Hindenburg*. We read about it in social studies last year."

"Inky, that happened ages ago."

I changed the subject: "My father's been gone for over a week. He's never stayed away that long."

"Has he phoned?"

"No."

"Does he usually phone?"

"Yes. He used to phone us every night when he was away. Now he usually calls if he's gone more than three days. It's been ten days."

The bus bumped along. We were silent. Other kids laughed and shouted. Caroline seemed about to cry. That's the kind of a friend she is.

"Have you noticed?" she asked softly. "I'm not making rhymes anymore."

I smiled and touched her hand briefly. "That's nice, Caroline. It was just a silly habit."

"Maybe it's not like you think," she said. "Maybe he really is with this man, his friend, and they are fishing."

"Or maybe this is the beginning of the end," I said. "It gets longer and longer. And pretty soon he'll decide, why bother coming home at all? I've been horrible to him, too."

"Inky, he loves you! Everyone knows your dad is the greatest. He spends time with you and does the neatest things with you. I bet he feels insecure. Maybe he just wants to know that people love him."

"He's always saying that," I murmured. I thought of his funny faces, his little boy smile: "Do ya love me just a little?"

"Does your mother tell him she loves him?"

"How would I know?"

"Well, you'd hear her, Inky. I hear my mother saying it all the time to my dad. Sometimes, in fact, they get way too mushy. I feel like I'm in the way."

"You mean, maybe if she told him," I pondered now, "if he realized she knew about it, and if she asked him to stop . . . ."

"That's it!" Caroline exclaimed. "I can see it now. It's probably all just a misunderstanding. He thinks she doesn't care. Doesn't love him. But she does, doesn't she?"

"Of course! She always fixes his favorite food when he comes home. She always says how great he is, bringing presents. I don't know what she'd do without him. They fight, sure, but they're really in love. I know they are!"

"You have to save the marriage," Caroline said solemnly.

I nodded.

"It's because she is so pure," Caroline said. "Your mom doesn't even suspect, because she's—well, you know."

I thought of my vision of her that day embroidering, how she sat there looking like a madonna. I knew what Caroline meant.

"She stays home so much," I said.

Caroline nodded. "So she doesn't realize."

"I see what you mean. How can I tell her?"

Caroline shrugged. We had come to my stop. "I don't know. Maybe you'll just know. It'll come to you. Don't worry."

But I did worry, all the way out to Shea Station.

Annie met me as usual, running in circles, leaping up to lick my face. Gus and I painted, while Mrs. McMurphy typed. It was getting to be like family. Like good friends. Too bad it would end after today.

Gus must have read my mind. "After we're done painting," he said, "why don't you come on back and help me fix the truck."

I looked up, exuberant. "What?"

"Yeah. I have to go over the engine. It's hard to have to reach for tools and things. You know."

"Sure," I said. "I'm terrific with engines." I started to laugh.

We finished the painting by four o'clock that afternoon. Gus took me out to the shed where he showed me the balloon. "You should see it up close," he said, "so you can paint it."

I looked at the basket with its instruments, the heavily padded railings, then at the bulky envelope in which the balloon was packed.

"Come over Sunday morning," Gus coaxed. "I'll take you up."

"No, Gus. I can't."

Annie, who had followed us, reared up at the sight of the basket and began to bark furiously, her fur ruffled, rump high in the air. I laughed and caught her in my arms. "Poor Annie!" I soothed. "You're scared to death of that thing, aren't you?"

"Animals usually are," Gus said. "Even the cows in the fields when we fly overhead—you should hear them mooing."

Annie licked my face, and I sat down with her in my lap.

"She never lies still that way," Gus said. "You have a special way with animals. Do you have a dog?"

"No. I used to have a tortoise, though." And I told Gus all about Roger. I'd never told anyone about Roger since he died, except in that essay.

"What was he like?" Gus wanted to know.

"You'll laugh, but he loved music. He'd get very still when I played records."

"What happened to him?"

"Oh," I chuckled, "he ran away and joined this new Rockabilly group, The Stir-Ups, in San Francisco."

"I suppose he plays the bass."

"Naturally."

"Let's sit in the basket," Gus said, climbing in, giving me his hand.

"That doesn't mean I'll go up, does it?"

Gus laughed. "Do you see any balloon attached? Woman, you are the most suspicious person! All I want you to do is sit here and tell me what happened to Roger."

I did. Gus listened soberly. "That's really rough," he said.

"Some people," I said, "don't think you can love a tortoise. Just because they're not furry and cuddly. But Roger knew me. He slept under my bed. He ate pizza crusts and lettuce. He was a wonderful pet."

"Why don't you get another one?"

"Can't. They don't import tortoises anymore. They're an endangered species. The only way you can get one is from another person who wants to give one up. They're very scarce. Besides . . . ."

"Besides, what?"

"I don't know," I said, but I did know, and I could tell Gus did, too. I wasn't eager to love another animal, to risk another loss.

We sat and talked about ballooning. Gus got his pilot's license when he was fifteen. Now he had a commercial license and could take people aloft.

"That's such a huge responsibility!" I exclaimed.

"Yes, it is. But I've had hundreds of hours of instruction."

"Is it hard?"

"It just takes practice. And, of course, you have to study the regulations. It wasn't hard for me. I wanted it more than anything. Especially after my . . . my dad tried ballooning first, you know. He was a daredevil, my dad. Wanted to go hang gliding, but Mom talked him out of it, got him a hot air balloon ride one morning, and that was it. Dad was hooked. Like I am now. Once you go up . . . ." Gus scanned the sky, as if to follow the soaring flight of birds. ". . . once you feel that sensation, you want to go aloft again and again."

I smiled. "So you end up buying your own balloon."

"Most people can just take it or leave it, do it once in a while for a lark. Then there are others. They live from ride to ride. It's an obsession. Know what I mean?" Gus said seriously.

"I guess so," I said slowly. "My little sister has an obsession," I said. "Unicorns."

"What's yours?"

"My father," I almost said, but instead, kept silent.

Gus went on. "When I go away to school, Mom's going to run the launch. Of course, Josh will be here to help, and some other people, I guess. Balloonists are the friendliest people in the world. That very first morning we ever went to the launch, everyone gave us a big smile; and next thing we knew, we were helping to hold her down. I was so scared and excited and . . . it makes a terrible racket when the blowers are on and the heat's going in. You should see it, Ingrid! That balloon gets bigger and lighter, and pretty soon it starts pulling, ready to take off on its own; you feel like yelling and laughing out loud. I did, watching my dad take off. Mom and I stood there and cheered, and she told me, 'This is it for him, Gus. I can feel it. Now everything will be different.'"

"Different?"

Gus shook his head, brushing away my question. "My dad was so excited! As if he had a new lease on life. He was like a little kid, laughing and carrying on. Oh, my dad used to laugh a lot. He was really fun when he wasn't . . . he had a terrific sense of humor."

I knew that Gus's father was dead, but none of the details. It didn't seem right to ask.

We got out of the basket and walked back to the house. Inside, Gus showed me a photograph of his first solo flight, mounted in the cover of a book about ballooning. I turned a page and saw a curious sketch.

"What's that?"

"A picture of the very first passengers to go up in a hot air balloon. It was in 1783, in France. Can you imagine how excited everyone was!"

"The passengers certainly look upset," I said pointing, giggling. Crowded into the gondola were a sheep, a rooster, and a duck. "They don't seem very happy at all."

"Well, the sheep got excited, and stepped on the rooster's wing and broke it," Gus explained. "The duck complained about the altitude. You can see he's very mad. But they made history. They started it all. Listen," Gus said softly, taking my hand. "If you come up with me on Sunday, I promise not to step on your wing. And you can make history, too."

"No. I can't." I tried to turn my gaze, but couldn't. I wanted to look into his eyes.

"You'd love it. Ingrid, it's the most exciting thing in the world. It's like floating in space, and the air is so pure; it's quiet up there, even colors are different. I promise you . . . ." Gus tightened his grasp on my hand. "You'll love it."

I pulled away. "I told you," I said curtly. "My father won't let me. He is very strict about things like that."

"If you disobey him," Gus began, "will he . . . ? I mean, does he hit you?"

"No. He never hits me. He's not like that."

"My father never hit me either," Gus said. "He was always joking and laughing, you know? We talked about going into the balloon business. But he . . . that was before he died. He never did get his license."

"But I thought you said he bought the balloon?"

Gus whirled around, his expression suddenly dark. "I never said that. Don't you think I know what I said?"

I'd never heard Gus use that tone before. I thought I heard a noise from the hall, or maybe I imagined that Mrs. McMurphy had been standing there listening, and that something about our conversation made her turn abruptly away.

WHEN I GOT HOME, my father's car was in the driveway.

My heart pounded as I entered the house. I dreaded seeing him, needed to see him, felt angry, and yet relieved. My legs trembled; too much bike riding, my mother would say.

He was cleaning his shoes out in the little washroom beyond the kitchen.

"Inky!" He smiled up at me. He looked marvelous, rested and tan, as usual after a time away. "I'm so sorry, I couldn't bring any gifts this time. There just wasn't any place . . . ."

"That's all right," I said. "I don't want any gifts." Only one gift, I thought. You. The way we used to be, before I knew. "How was your trip?" I asked. "Did you catch any fish?"

"Not many. The few we got, we gave to the guides. They need them for food."

"That was kind of you." He did not notice the sarcasm in my tone.

"Well, we do what we can."

"Were you worried about us while you were gone?"

"Why should I worry?" he countered.

"Anything could happen. I read in the paper two women got struck by lightning during a freak storm, just thirty miles from here. Anything can happen," I repeated.

"Well, I trust your mother to take care of things."

"I'm sure she trusts you, too." I said pointedly.

I don't know what I was looking for. A confession? A change. Something to make us all better. Closer. Safe.

"How's school?" he asked, putting away the polish and brushes.

"Oh, terrific."

Becca came running in. "Hi, baby!" my father called. "Seen any unicorns lately?"

"Not lately," she replied, smiling. "Have you?"

"Well, late one night I happened to peek out of the cabin, sweetheart, and it seems to me I saw something flashing, like the golden horn of a beautiful, incredible beast. Could have been a unicorn, I suppose. Yes, it certainly could have been."

"Unicorns don't live at the beach, Daddy," Becca admonished.

I left. Men, I thought in disgust, the same tone I'd heard before many times. Men! Soon I heard the shower, the familiar singing, everything about the same as always. But not quite.

In the kitchen my mother was washing up some pots, sighing over a broken cup.

"Don't you have any homework to do?" she greeted me.

"I've done most of it." Actually, I'd done nothing.

"You can help me with these pots if you don't mind," she said sharply. "I get tired to death doing everything around here myself."

"Aren't you glad Daddy's back?"

"Of course I am."

"He was gone for ten days."

"Yes. I can count." She had cut her finger and now searched in the drawer for a bandage.

"Did you miss him?"

"Inky, for heaven's sake, why must you pester me with a million questions all the time? What's the matter with you? Are you upset because, for once, your father didn't bring you a present? Is that it?"

"Why don't you and father ever go on vacations together?"

"Are you going to start that again? Inky, I'm in no mood for it. Anyway, don't you remember? We all went to Orange County last summer for the whole weekend."

"That's not what I mean! I mean just the two of you, alone together."

"Well, of course, we did that before you girls were born. We went on a honeymoon, and we went other places, too. Yosemite, once. And we went to Salt Lake City for his brother's wedding."

"Barbara's parents went to Hawaii. Just the two of them. When they came back, Barbara says they were all starry-eyed."

"Don't you girls keep anything private? My heavens." She chuckled. "I'd hate to think what her folks would say if they heard you."

"Do you and Daddy still sleep together?"

"My God, Inky, what sort of a question is that?"

"I mean sex. Do you ever have sex anymore?"

She plunged the roasting pan into the dishwater with such force that a wave surged out over the sink and onto the floor. Dirty, soapy water slopped over the front of my mother's dress. Her face became red, and her eyes pink rimmed, like a rabbit's.

"What a mess!" my mother screamed. "Every time you come into this kitchen, it's a disaster. I'd rather do it myself, believe me. If you cared anything for me . . . if you had half an ounce of consideration . . . ."

"I care for you," I said. "I am only trying to help you. Who do you think took that flight bag?"

Mother turned to me, her face ashen. Her dress, still soaking wet, lay plastered against her thighs.

"Your father's flight bag? What are you talking about?"

"I took it," I said. "I had to. It was for you."

"Ingrid! How could you do such a thing? My God, your father will . . . ."

We turned simultaneously to see him standing in the doorway.

13

"WHAT ON EARTH is going on here?" my father demanded. My mother shivered in her wet dress, and I stood waiting for everything to come crashing down. She'd tell him I stole the flight bag.

"Nothing, Peter. Nothing, really."

"I heard you say something about my flight bag."

"Oh. Yes. Well, how about some crackers and cheese? A little appetizer? We have fresh cheddar."

"All right. Why not."

My mother rushed to get it. "Promise me you won't get upset," she began.

"I never get upset." He nibbled a cracker. "Unless it's justified."

"Well, I want you to keep this in perspective, Peter. The most important thing is for us all to get along. I don't want you to be angry with Mama. She's an old woman. She tries her best, but . . . ."

"What did she do now?" My father cut a wedge of cheese with a single motion.

"I'll tell you, provided you say nothing to her about it. Promise me, Peter. Will you promise?"

I held my breath.

"How can I promise something when I don't know about it?"

"I don't want you to yell at her. Or do anything you'll be sorry for. After all, she is your mother. And she adores you."

Father shook his head, and smiled indulgently. "You. You always take her side. All right. What is it now?"

"It's about that flight bag you're missing—she gave a bunch of stuff to the Goodwill while you were gone, including that bag. She told me it was torn, so she thought it was no good. I don't think she even opened it."

"It was just some old travel folders and brochures," my father said. "I don't care about that. It's the principle."

"I know, I know," my mother soothed. "But what's done is done. I'll try to watch her more closely in future. I'll keep her out of your den. Just don't say anything to her. She'll feel that I broke a confidence, and then she'll be angry with me, and it will be so hard . . . ."

"All right, Marguerite. You can't stand strife, can you, Marguerite?" He gazed at her for a moment more. "But how did you get so wet? You're soaked."

"I dropped something into the dishwater."

"What was it, a whale?" They both laughed.

I went into Grandma's room, my novel under my arm. Mrs. Ebert had made a bargain with me; I was supposed to have finished the book by the end of next week.

Grandma was knitting, listening to her tiny TV set, which my father bought her for Christmas last year. It is much too small for her poor eyes, but Grandma always says she doesn't need to see the screen; she only likes to hear the sound.

"Want me to read to you?" I asked.

"Oh, I'd love that," she said. "But don't turn off the TV."

"All right." I was used to reading over the sound. Now I began, without explaining the first part of the story. Grandma didn't mind. She enjoyed the sound of my voice, she always said. I read on and on to the rapid movement of her knitting needles and the droning of the TV.

Soon Grandma seemed lost in the story; I knew it was only the sound of my voice, and that the plot meant nothing to her. I asked softly, "Grandma, what was my mother like before she married Dad?"

"Well, they met when she was at her cousin's, you know, in Monterey. We were living there then. She was a pretty little thing. Like you are now."

"Grandma, I'm not the least bit pretty."

Grandma looked at me in amazement. "Why, you *are*, Ingrid. Sure, you aren't little, but you are very pretty.

Your skin. Your eyes and your hair; I think you are a beautiful girl."

"And Mama was beautiful?"

"Why, she still is. Your father certainly thinks so."

"Then why does he . . . ." I bit my lip hard. "Why doesn't he ever say so?"

"He doesn't have to *say* it. He brings her a present every time he comes home."

"Why don't you like presents, Grandma?"

"Your father has too many expenses as it is," she replied. "He shouldn't be spending extra money on me."

I put down my book and sat close beside Grandma, on a thick cushion at her feet. I wanted to clasp her knees, to put my head down in her lap, but I knew that too great a show of emotion would push Grandma back into silence. I whispered, "Why did they get married? They don't like any of the same things."

"They get along," Grandma said. "It's always a mystery, what makes a marriage work. Not for us to inquire." The finished patch of beige wool lay on her lap, and she stroked it while she spoke. "Your father was such a gadabout! Really, a wild boy. I spoiled him. I know that. But he was my only child, and a son, and I . . . . Marguerite was a sweet little thing, and shy. She loved to sit and listen to him speak to her, read to her, take her to the movies."

"Then why won't she go anywhere with him now?"

"Why must she? Why *should* she? Your mama is content here in her house, with her garden and her two girls.

Besides, she takes care of me. Why should she do anything more?"

"Because he . . . he likes to go out," I said in desperation. "He likes to be active. She just stays inside . . . ."

"A man likes a woman to come home to," said my grandmother. She picked up a ball of navy blue yarn and began to knit again. "I have to concentrate now, Ingrid. Don't talk."

"Grandma." She bent over her work, concentrating as if her life depended on it. "Grandma, why does he get so angry? Was he always that way?"

She gazed up at me, her eyes seeming opaque, suddenly, her mood transformed. "I don't know what you're talking about. Peter is a good boy. He takes care of his mother. He never leaves me alone. I will always have a home here with my son."

I went to my room, remembering that old story about the blind men and the elephant. Each blind man touches a different part of the elephant and believes he knows everything about it, when in fact, he knows only a part of the truth.

M RS. E BERT called me up to her desk one day after class. "I want to talk to you, Ingrid," she said. "Your grades have been skidding down for the past month. I can't help thinking that there has to be a reason. A bright girl like you, grades suddenly falling, daydreaming in class. What's wrong, Ingrid?"

"I can't help my personality, Mrs. Ebert," I said, low and a little hostile.

"We're not talking about personality, Ingrid, but school performance. Usually a change like this indicates some kind of problem. Something that we can get help with."

We. That's what they always say when they want to dig into your life, your soul. We—as if they were sharing anything.

"Sometimes we need someone to talk to, Ingrid, to help sort things out. Everyone has problems. All problems are surmountable, with help."

"I don't have any problems," I said, looking down at my hands, thinking I would get some polish for my nails. Bright red. Like Judy Treehoff wore. Maybe I'd color my hair, too, just in the front, maybe a lavender curl.

When I got home my mother was out on the porch watching for me, a bad sign. She called out, "Where's your sister?"

"At Tina's." I turned toward the garage.

"Ingrid! Just a minute, young lady."

"What's wrong?"

"Don't yell across the yard. Come here. And forget about going anywhere on your bicycle. I just had a call from your teacher, Mrs. Ebert. She says you are getting a "D" in English."

I shrugged. "English isn't my best subject," I said. "I try."

"That's not what I hear from Mrs. Ebert. You don't do the assignments; you haven't read that book; you daydream in class."

"She's wrong," I said with another shrug.

"I do not like teachers calling me up to tell me you are failing!"

"'D' isn't failure. It means barely passing. I don't like the books she assigns. You wouldn't either. They're boring."

"Ingrid, you have to do your work. Mrs. Ebert asked me to come to the school," my mother went on. "You know how I feel about that. Inky? Don't you?"

"Yes," I said softly.

"You know how I feel about strangers interfering in family business. I don't want to have to be called in to see your teacher, as if I were guilty of something, do you understand? Now, sweetheart, listen. I know it isn't always fun doing homework. I know school can be an awful bore. But you've got to try. Please, honey. Just read that book. Then we won't have to hear anything more about it. All right?"

"All right."

"That's my good girl."

"Can I go now, Mom?"

"Where are you going?"

"I thought I'd go over to McClures. I need some new pencils."

"Then you can do me a favor and buy me some embroidery thread. Any shade of pink. I've been needing it for a week."

I sighed. Mom won't go into McClure's since one of the sales ladies sassed her a year ago, and the manager refused to fire the woman.

"All right." I'd have to hurry and get the thread first. I pulled my bicycle out of the garage, aching to be gone toward Gus's.

"Inky!" Mom called out. "Be careful, darling. I love you. If you go to Caroline's, be home before dark."

I felt guilty. It was getting to be my usual feeling. I raced to McClures, then sped along the tar road so fast my legs got cramped and I had to slow down.

At last I saw the display balloon, bobbing just beyond Gus's house. I raced up the steps, and even before Annie could reach the door with her barking, I banged on it calling, "Gus! Gus!"

Mary McMurphy came running. "Good grief, what's the matter, Ingrid? You gave me such a scare. Gus isn't here."

"Not here?"

Mrs. McMurphy drew me inside. "You look white as a sheet," she said. "What happened?"

"I—nothing. I get this way sometimes. A slight case of anemia, I think."

"Ah, well, let me give you some good medicine. Oatmeal cookies with raisins. Raisins provide iron, did you know that? And a cold glass of milk. Sit down, Ingrid.

Gus will be back soon. He went off to Castle for some auto parts."

"Can he really fix the truck?"

"Oh, yes. Gus is very mechanical." She chuckled. "From the time Gus was two years old, it became apparent that he was the only one in the family who could put things together. Clocks, our old radio, motors. Both his dad and I were all thumbs. Notice, I said 'were.' After my husband died, I had to learn. Oh, boy, did I. Lots of things."

"Like balloon launching?"

"Yes, like balloon launching. And learning how to live without . . . ." Mary McMurphy reached up, pulled the clip out of her hair and let it fall, giving her head a shake. "Without guilt. You know, when someone dies, it's natural to feel guilty."

"Oh, yes," I said quickly. "I know that."

"Because," she continued rapidly, "nobody is perfect. When a person dies, we are free of their faults, too. So we feel relieved. Almost glad. Then our conscience bothers us. So we feel guilty." She took a deep breath, then smiled at me. "The preceding lecture," she said with a grin, "is the result of about six months of therapy. So. How's that sign coming along?"

"I'm working on it."

"Good." Mary McMurphy smiled. "Take your time, but hurry up. How are the cookies?"

"Great," I said, with my mouth full.

She took one and ate it all, then took another. I liked the fact that she wasn't talking about calories, just enjoying the cookies. "Delicious," she said with a grin. "Even though I made them myself."

"Gus says you're a very good cook."

"He does? Well, bless his heart. All his compliments are indirect. He doesn't want me to get conceited."

"You're not."

"Does it bother you a lot?" she suddenly asked, her blue eyes very warm, very serious. "Your mother, I mean." She did not touch me, but I felt as if she had. "You were so young. And what about your sister? Who takes care of her? It must be very hard."

"It is. But then," I said, "my father is really terrific. He takes us places, and he plays with us and helps me with my homework. Whenever he has vacations, Becca and I go somewhere special with him. Next spring he's going to take us to Mexico deep-sea fishing. Maybe over Christmas we'll go to Hawaii. It's really O.K. See, my mother was always sick. So it was for the best that she died. Really. She's at peace now."

Mary McMurphy nodded. "That's what I have to tell myself about Ray. My husband. That he's at peace now. It was always such a struggle for him. I mean, with the drinking and all."

I sat frozen. "Drinking?"

"Didn't Gus tell you?"

"Not much," I said.

"I thought he would have told you. You see, we both decided not to hide from it. We went to Al-Anon. That's a group for the families of alcoholics. Because, finally, we had to admit that's what he was. An alcoholic. When he drank, he changed completely. That last time he hit Gus so hard I thought he'd broken his jaw."

"Hit? Hit him?"

"I'd always gone to look for Ray before that. I'd find him at a friend's house, or some broken-down hotel. Then I'd clean him up and take him home, and he'd make a hundred promises, none of which he could keep. But I kept thinking he'd change, and he kept making promises. We were playing each other's game: He falling apart with the alcohol; I running out to save him— until that last time. When he hurt Gus so badly, I had to make a decision. I didn't go looking for him. And when he came back, I said we didn't want him. Unless he could fight it and lick it."

Mrs. McMurphy looked at me intently.

"I think you did the right thing," I said solemnly. I'd never felt so close to a woman before. It was almost as if, somehow, we were the same age, or that age didn't matter.

"Hey, what's going on? I smell cookies, a party." It was Gus, banging the door behind him.

"How's it going?" he greeted me, reaching for several cookies.

"Fine. Ingrid and I were just talking. Girl talk."

"Oh, really?" Gus grinned. "About what?"

"Men, naturally." We both laughed.

Gus turned to me. "Ingrid, want to help me with the truck?"

I glanced at Mrs. McMurphy; we shared a secret smile. "Oh, sure, Gus. I'm great with motors."

"I thought you would be. Come on!" He took the box of parts, and we went outside, where he began immediately tinkering with the motor, while I stood by handing him tools.

At last Gus put the tools away and, after wiping his hands, reached for two sodas, tossing one to me.

"You're terrific," he said. "We're a great team."

"Thank you, Gus." I watched him closely, trying to figure him out. He had told me how terrific his father was, yet the man had beaten him. At least my father never did that. He never laid a hand on us.

I had to say something. "Your mother told me about your dad," I began. "How he hurt you. I'm really sorry."

"He didn't mean to hit me!" Gus shouted, belligerent now. "It was an accident."

"O.K. I just wanted to say—I'm sorry. About everything."

"There's nothing to be sorry about!" he cried. "My dad just died. Lots of people do. Your mother did. It happens."

"Gus!" Mary McMurphy stood in the doorway, behind the screen. Her features were stern. "Don't do that, Gus. Ingrid is your friend. Don't do it to her or to yourself."

"Leave me alone, Mom!" Gus cried.

"Gus, we decided together, we agreed . . . ."

"Leave me alone!" he shouted again, and with a leap he was off the porch and into the truck, gunning the motor and speeding away down the desert road.

14

✴

THAT NIGHT I phoned Caroline. "I guess it's over between me and Gus," I told her.

"Why?" she breathed. "What happened? Did you have a fight?"

"He's been lying to me," I said. "Isn't that a laugh? And I was so worried about what I told him. Actually," I said, feeling a dreadful ache in my chest, "it's O.K. I mean, it was getting to be too heavy."

"Because he's older?"

"He's going to college next term."

"So, are you going to try to get Buzz back?"

"Caroline, I never had anything but one single date with Buzz Duarte. Anyhow, he's going with Judy Treehoff."

"Well, you're a lot cuter," Caroline said. "Everybody thinks Judy Treehoff is a tramp."

"Maybe she isn't really," I said. I felt sorry for Judy, suddenly.

"They picked Roadrunner today," Caroline told me. "The other two contenders dropped out. It's Tracy Costas."

Another blow. I'd been hoping to screw up my courage to try it, maybe next week. Too late.

"I hated to have to tell you," Caroline said.

"It's all right. Really. This just isn't my week. Or my month, either. Mrs. Ebert called my mom today. Wants her to come for a conference."

"Did you talk to your mom?"

"No." I didn't explain. I was chicken. The time never seemed right, and I didn't know the right words.

That weekend I hung around the house. Caroline was gone for a tennis meet over in San Bernardino. It was a whole weekend-long event, with schools from all over southern California participating. It made me wish more than ever that I'd tried out for Roadrunner. Then, I could have been there. I was restless and filled with regret.

I noticed, as I tried to read or sketch or practice soccer moves with Becca, that my father was restless, too. He stood by the window looking out, like a prisoner. He went down to the mall, engaged Becca in games, asked me to go target shooting with him. I have never liked

37

the target range; this time I told him so.

He seemed crushed. "I thought I could count on you," he said.

"I'm sorry. I get ill at the range. The shooting gives me a headache."

He raised his brows, said nothing, continued to stare out the window, then remained in his den most of the day Sunday.

"I'm thinking of asking for a different run," he told Mother that evening.

"Oh? Where to?" asked Mom, and Grandma only smiled and patted down her hair.

"Something different," he said. "I'm getting incredibly bored doing the same thing year after year. I thought of going international, but . . . ."

My heart sank. International meant changes. Vast changes. Longer separations, stopovers in foreign lands, a different airline; maybe we'd even have to move.

"Where were you thinking of?"

"The Orient," said my father.

"I would hate to have to eat Oriental food," said my mother.

"Well, I know you don't ever eat foreign foods, Marguerite," he said pleasantly. "But for some of us, variety is the spice of life."

"You can get a terrible stomach virus from eating raw fish," my mother said. "Of course," she smiled at him, "it's entirely up to you. To each his own."

"Yes, indeed," said my father. He wiped his lips carefully, and meticulously folded his napkin and laid it down beside his plate.

"Then you have no objections?" he asked.

My mother shrugged. "What right have I to object? It's your career. Your decision. I've never stood in your way, Peter. You know that."

He stood up. "Sweet Marguerite," he said, and I heard the shade of sarcasm in his tone. My mother, on the other hand, merely began to clear the table and announced brightly, "Apple cobbler for dessert. Who wants whipped cream on it?"

When my father left again, I felt relieved, yet anxious. He would be making inquiries, making plans that would include all of us. How could Mom be so unconcerned?

"I'll never leave Seven Wells," I heard my mother telling Grandma as she helped her change her linen. "Don't you worry, Mama. I belong here, and this is where I'll stay."

I heard muffled words, high pitched and worried.

I sat at my desk, tortured by indecision. Tell Mom! Keep still. It was like a war inside my head. I didn't even hear the telephone. Becca came rushing into my room. "It's for you, Inky. It's a boy!"

Boys don't usually call me. I ran out to the hall and held the receiver for a long moment before I spoke. "Hello."

"Hello, Ingrid. Please don't be mad at me for calling

you at home. I know you said your dad doesn't like you to tie up the telephone, but . . . ."

"It's all right, Gus. My father's not here."

"Oh. Was that your little sister who answered the phone?"

"Yes."

"She sounded cute. And nice. Like you."

I stood there, numb. He'd called! I couldn't think of a thing to say. "How's Annie?" I asked.

"She misses you," Gus said smoothly. "We were wondering whether you'd like to come over and see us. How about tomorrow? It's Saturday."

"Saturday? Saturday." I felt tongue-tied, almost dizzy.

"I was hoping you could come over and—eh—help me with the truck."

I heard a groan in the background.

"That is," he said, "just come on over and let's have a picnic, O.K.?"

"I'd love to."

"Great. See you. Hey, that's great."

Becca was waiting for me on my bed, grinning. "Who was that?"

"Just a boy I know," I said, unable to conceal a smile.

"Are you going on a date?"

"Promise not to tell?"

"Cross my heart and hope to die, stick a needle in my eye."

"He asked me to go on a picnic tomorrow."

"Can I come?"

"No! Of course not. Remember," I added hastily, "you promised. You swore."

"I never tell on you," Becca said.

"What do you mean? What would you tell?"

"That you go out into the desert," Becca said solemnly. "I've known about it for a long time. I've seen you ride off."

"Are you going to tell Mom?"

"No."

"Becca," I said, "I'm not doing anything bad. He's really nice, and he's got a terrific home and a wonderful mom. They run the balloon launch. That truck we saw on Halloween? That was his."

"Wowee." Becca's eyes were wide. "Are you going to go up in the balloon?"

"Don't I wish I could?" I said bitterly. "He's asked me. So has his mom. I'm supposed to make a poster for them, and they said they'll take me up. Up. It sounds so simple."

"I'll go instead," Becca offered.

"Forget it!" I gave her a swat. "Remember. It's a secret."

"How will you get out?"

"I'll think of a way." Overcome with joy, I sang out, "Tomorrow! Tomorrow!"

"I hate tomorrow," said Becca, brooding.

"What's wrong?"

"Soccer. Tomorrow's the first day for sign-ups. Tina

and Nonie are going to be mad at me if I don't sign up. They won't be friends with me anymore."

"Silly," I scolded, tossing my head impatiently. "You don't have to play soccer to stay friends with them. You do whatever you want. Tell them you can't. Tell them to have to stay home on Saturdays and help take care of Grandma."

Instantly Becca brightened. "I could do that, couldn't I? Inky, you're a genius."

"Anytime."

In the morning I cleaned my room, then grabbed my book bag and told my mother I was going to the library to work on a report.

"How in the world are you getting clear over to Castle?" she asked.

"I'm riding my bike to Caroline's. Her mother is taking us. I'll be back way before dinner."

"Well, that's fine, Inky. Have a nice day." Mom smiled at me.

I wanted to throw my arms around her; I wanted so much to tell her about Gus. But I didn't dare. She'd find some objection I knew. Everything would be over.

Gus had washed the truck; new seatcovers concealed the worn spots, and the chrome was polished.

"I thought we'd drive over to Ross Meadows," Gus said. "Mom packed us a fabulous lunch. Fried chicken and fixings."

"Is your mom coming with us?"

Gus laughed. "No. Just us two. Do you mind?"

"I don't mind."

"Then step into my golden coach!" Gus opened the truck door and gave me his arm to boost me up the high step.

Gus put the basket down on the floor by my feet, then got in. Mary McMurphy came to the door, holding Annie by the collar. The dog strained and wriggled, barking and yelping.

Gus shot a questioning glance at me.

"Let her come," I said.

"It's O.K.!" Gus shouted. "Annie, come on!"

With a leap Annie was in the back of the truck, and we took off, bumping along the gravel road until we hit the highway. I had ridden on that highway a hundred times at least. But never never like this, sitting up high in the truck beside Gus. I wanted to sing. I wanted to make my own new song. Gus turned on the radio. Suddenly, we were both singing out loud, then laughing when the song ended.

"I discovered Lake Ross just the other day," Gus said. "Have you been there?"

"Once or twice," I said. "When I was little."

"With your folks?"

"Yes. We fed the ducks there. We walked around. It was pretty."

"You didn't picnic?"

"No. My mother was there, too. She doesn't—didn't like to eat outdoors. She had a lot of—of things she wouldn't do."

"Well, I guess that's because she was sick. When you're in pain, or not feeling well, you don't like to do things."

"She wasn't in pain," I said. "She was just—she never went out much. Even when she was well. She was scared of crowds."

"Maybe she had agoraphobia," Gus said.

We had come to the picnic ground by Lake Ross. Gus pulled the truck in under some trees. I could smell the leaves, that rich, damp fragrance. Some were turning gold; the pines were thick and full with greenery, the ground soft with pine needles. Ahead, the small lake showed sparkling silver patches through the trees.

Annie jumped out of the truck, sniffing at the ground, her tail wagging madly.

A few hikers were about, as well as a family with three little children, and an elderly couple quietly sitting on beach chairs in the shade, reading newspapers.

"Want to eat first?" Gus asked. "Or walk."

"Let's walk around the lake," I said, eager, my heart beating swiftly as I went ahead toward the path that circumscribes the water. I had walked here once before, that time years ago, with Daddy and Becca, and I remembered wading in the water and looking for bread crusts to feed the ducks that waddle and quack at the edge. Those same ducks—or their relatives—were there now, quacking loudly, fluttering their feathers and creating their small, colorful flurries of excitement.

"I love the ducks," I said. Gus walked close beside

me on the narrow path. Our steps coincided exactly.

Annie ran ahead, then turned back to see that we were coming, mouth open, grinning with pleasure at this outing.

"I brought some hot dogs for Annie," Gus said.

"Oh? You were that sure I'd want her along?"

"Yup. In fact, I figured that was the main reason you were going. You and she are pals, aren't you?"

"That's right. Annie and I. You're just along as the driver."

Gus took my hand, and we walked along, just holding hands. It was the most dazzling sensation I had ever known, the warmth of his hand, the strength, the feeling of being linked to somebody else, for no reason except that you enjoyed touching.

"What is agoraphobia?" I asked.

"Fear of going out," Gus said. "I don't know a lot about it. I read an article, though. Some people have it so bad they can't leave their house at all."

"What happens when they do?"

"They panic. I guess it's a terrible fear. I read this book on abnormal psychology, all about phobias. It's really interesting."

"Are you saying my mother wasn't normal?"

"Hey, hold it! I'm not criticizing your mother. You asked me about phobias. I think they sort of grow on a person. First you won't go out in big crowds, or very far from home. The fear gets worse, I suppose, every time you give in to it. It's like," he paused, "like any addiction."

"You mean, like bad habits?"

He nodded. "When I was eight, I used to have to fold up every little piece of string I found. I mean, I *had* to. If there was a piece of string on the street, I'd go back, pick it up and fold it, even if it was dirty or wet. Then I started with other stuff, like the bathroom towels and papers and clothes."

"You mean, folding things up is a phobia?"

Gus frowned. "No. A phobia is when you *can't* do something. A fear that doesn't really make sense. But when you *have* to do something it's called a compulsion. I mean, I just couldn't help myself. I'd get really nervous, so I'd start folding things, and pretty soon I just *had* to do it. A thing like that gets to be a habit. And it controls you."

"So how do people get over it?"

Gus shrugged. "Different ways. With me, I was just really scared all the time when I was little. My mom got me some help. She also got me into Little League baseball. I got busier and busier. Also the coach and I became very good friends."

I'm nothing like that, I thought to myself. I don't fold things. I'm not afraid to go places.

Gus continued, "The coach took me out and spent time with me. See, my father was . . . ." Gus looked straight at me. "My father was an alcoholic. He got mean when he drank. He kept promising to quit, but he couldn't. He beat me up. Lots of times. The worst thing was, I never knew what to expect."

We had come back to the picnic grounds. We moved toward the benches, and I kept silent, astonished at his honesty.

"Alcoholics can be . . . the thing is, when he was sober, my dad was the greatest. When he drank, he changed completely. We had to—to learn how to deal with it. To face it. If people ignore their problems, they come out in other ways." Gus chuckled, but coldly. "Like folding up string and things. The thing is, like they taught us at Al-Anon, if one person is sick it affects the whole family."

I listened. I couldn't say a word.

"The thing was, the hard thing . . ." Gus wiped his forehead with his hand, ". . . when my dad died, he'd been sober for nearly a year. That's what was so sad. Drinking had affected his health." Gus shrugged. "I just wanted you to know. He never bought the balloon, because he was already dead. Mom and I decided to buy it. To go into business. It was a big risk. We had to use some of the insurance money."

We fed Annie the hot dogs. I nibbled at the chicken and corn muffins, watching Gus as he ate, thinking how wonderful he was. I'd never really loved a boy before.

"I want to change," I heard myself saying suddenly.

Gus stared at me, then broke into a smile. Swiftly he came near, put his arm around me, gave me a light kiss on the lips. "Don't change too much," he said. "I like you the way you are."

"I have fears," I told Gus, as we munched the apples

his mom had packed, sipping our soda pop, both leaning against the same wide tree trunk, not touching, except for our arms, just slightly. "I've always been afraid of heights."

"Even babies are afraid of high places," Gus said. "It's instinctive."

"How come you know everything?" I was only half teasing.

"I read a lot," Gus said. "It's a consequence of being kicked out of school."

"Come on. You don't mean it."

"Oh, yes. I told you I was a rowdy kid."

"What'd you do?"

"It was after my father died. I couldn't handle it. I just started fighting a lot. Acting out. The principal and my mom thought it would be better for me to take time off. I was sixteen. So I went to work. Also, we needed the money. My mom was in bad shape, too. I got one job at a gas station, and another, weekends, being a guide with this tour group that takes people camping. That's what I really want to do."

"I thought you wanted to be in the balloon business."

"You can't do that year round. But," Gus said, with that gleam in his eyes, "I have thought about going into the recreation business: balloon rides, river rafting trips, back-packing. My mom and I have it all figured out. She'll do the catering for our trips; I'll be the guide."

"Do you know about river rafting?"

"Some. I'll learn more. And I'll study business in college, too, so we can handle our own advertising and accounts. Maybe we can do camping trips all over the world. I'd love to travel."

"My father travels a lot. It's not so great."

"It will be different for me," Gus said. "What are your plans? Do you know what you want to do?"

I smiled, squinting against the sun. "Nobody's ever asked me that before," I said. "I like to sketch and paint. I'd love to see the Colorado River. But what I really love the most is the zoo. You know, being with the animals. Taking care of them. Fixing their habitats. I like taking care of things." My voice rose. I had never talked about this before to anyone. "I think it's cruel the way we keep animals in zoos. I want to change that."

"Get rid of zoos?" Gus seemed surprised.

"No. Make them different. Better. With activities for the animals."

"Dances, you mean? Concerts?" Gus laughed.

"Maybe," I retorted, laughing too. "That's not a bad idea. Animals love music. A concert at the zoo would be a great idea."

We took the left-over hot dog buns and fed them to the ducks. Annie kept her distance, and Gus teased her. "You're not very brave, Annie," he chided.

"Neither am I," I said.

"Is that why you won't go up in our balloon? Fear of heights?"

I nodded. "I'll never get over it."

"You might."

"How?"

"Sometimes just talking about it helps. The group my mom and I went to taught us to talk about feelings instead of keeping them inside. Everyone's got problems."

I thought of Mrs. Ebert.

We gathered up our things and walked back to the truck. "Gus," I said, "do you think agoraphobia is inherited?"

"No. No way. I think people can decide how they want to be. I think they can work on it."

I wanted to work on it. And I wanted to tell Gus. But I didn't know how to begin. Maybe actions, I thought, are better than words.

15

IT WAS SATURDAY NIGHT. Becca had gotten permission to stay overnight at Tina's. Grandma was asleep in her chair, rocking slightly; we could hear the faint sounds from her room, comfortable and easy.

The rocker creaked gently, while in the living room I was ironing my blouses, and Mother sat before the television set embroidering. The television movie was mere background noise for us both. My mother's expression was one of utmost concentration as she neatly stitched.

We'd all had such a nice time at dinner. Mom got us pizza with pepperoni on it, my favorite, and for dessert, I had made chocolate pudding. Now I could smell the sweet jasmine from the open window. The old parchment shade on the brass table lamp gave a golden glow to the room.

The program ended. The news came on. I knew my mom wouldn't want to watch the late night news; she says it's depressing. I turned off the TV set.

I glanced over at her. She was wearing my favorite shirt, bright pink and belted at the waist. She looked young and pretty, and she wore her white sandals instead of her old scuffs.

"I have something to tell you," I heard myself saying, although I barely recognized the voice.

"Oh? Can it wait until tomorrow?" My mother yawned. "I think I'd like to go to bed."

"It can't wait any longer," I said. "If I wait, I might chicken out. And I have to tell you."

My mother smiled and reached out to touch my cheek. "Inky, you are always so dramatic. You and Becca both. What is it, child?"

"I have to tell you about the flight bag," I said, muffled, avoiding her eyes. "I took it. I guess I was scared you'd find it. I don't know."

"Look, Inky," my mother said calmly. "As far as your father's concerned, the matter is closed. It was naughty of you to take something of his. But the fact is, you were lucky. He doesn't need that bag, and it's all forgotten. So stop feeling guilty. It's all right. We all make mistakes."

"There's more," I said. I seemed to have trouble breathing; suddenly the jasmine enveloped me like a closed net.

"More confessions, Inky?"

Something in my mother's attitude made me think

she already knew what I was going to say. A dozen ideas crossed my mind; she knew, already knew. So it was O.K. Somehow, it was O.K. Like the time I lost my new sweater when I was seven, and cried to confess it, but she already knew, had found it at the supermarket, and it was O.K.

"That night Caroline was here," I began, and moistened my lips, "and we went into Daddy's den . . . we were looking for paper. But I happened to open his flight bag. And I saw all these letters, Mom, letters from friends of his."

She nodded slowly. I could read nothing in her expression.

"One was from a lady I had met when we were in San Francisco. I'd thought she was very nice. Very pretty, you know. Her name was Alissa James."

"You have a good memory, Inky," my mother said, and still her tone revealed nothing. "What is the point?" Her eyes, now, were keen, holding me to account.

"Well, the point is, I took the letter, because I thought . . . I know I shouldn't have been snooping, but . . . ."

"Exactly right," Mother said sharply. "You did not belong in your father's den, much less poking into his private possessions."

"I know that, Mom, I know that," I cried, feeling stiffled again, held down by the heavy smell of jasmine, by the heat of my own skin, by shame. "But I— saw the letter and I took it, and I read it and it was a . . . a letter like . . . you know like you read about? It was . . . I don't know, Mom, how to say it . . . she said she loved him. She said she loved Daddy!"

Nothing happened. No trace of feeling crossed my mother's face. She simply stood there, her arms slightly out from her sides, breathing in and out, steady and controlled.

"Your father is a good-looking man," she said softly. "Naturally, women find him attractive." She turned, as if to dismiss it now. "Is that the big deal, my dear? If so, don't worry about it any more. You really are awfully dramatic, sweetheart. It isn't always a good way to be."

"That isn't all!" I cried, wanting to pull her back, to make her see without having to speak the words. But she did not see, could not imagine, needed to be told, and so I closed my eyes, and through sobs the words came out, halting and mixed up I suppose, unclear but clear enough so that when I was finished I remember the jumbled echoes of my own words, thrown out like sharp stones every which way . . . "so many other women . . . pictures, love letters . . . meeting them in hotels, do you understand? He lies to us, Mama! He lies to us all the time!"

I opened my eyes to see that she had not moved at all, but stood there watching me as if I were a creature out of control, doing some wild and crazy dance that must find its own end.

"Mom! Didn't you hear me? Why won't you say something? I took the bag. I didn't know what to do! I wanted to tell you, Mom, all these weeks, but I didn't know how. I'm sorry, I'm sorry, but I thought you would need to know, because maybe if you talk to him about it honestly, then things can change. I mean, people have problems, but unless they talk about them . . . ." I caught my breath, holding back tears. "Maybe you could work it out."

A long silence filled the room. I could hear a bird outside, singing heartily, as if it were daybreak, when in fact it was near midnight.

"You want me to work it out," my mother said. She turned and went to the sofa, where she sat down. I followed.

"Sit down, Inky," she said. "No! Not beside me. Sit over there, where I can look at you."

I took the chair opposite. Something in her voice made me afraid. Is this my mother? I thought. Maybe not, came the crazy idea; maybe she really isn't my mother at all, but I was adopted as a baby, and she'll tell me so now—but what difference would that make? Nothing made sense.

"First of all," she said, "I know all about Alissa James."

"You *know*?" I breathed. "You know her?"

"Oh, we've never met. But I know she owns a lovely shop in San Francisco. Your father bought me my Christmas present from that shop last year. They have known each other for years. They are good friends."

I shook my head. "Mom. That letter . . . ."

"You don't understand these things, Inky. Believe me,

when you are older, you will understand. Ingrid," she said, "you are still a child. Much too young for us to be having such a discussion. But you blundered into this, and you might as well learn it: Men are not like women. Not at all. Their needs are not the same."

"You mean they all cheat?"

She did not even wince, but sat there calm, gazing to a point above me, beyond me.

"I'm not worried about your father, Ingrid. Really, I'm not. The one I'm worried about is you. What kind of a girl is it who goes sneaking behind her father's back, taking his things? What kind of a child goes running to her mother, bearing ugly tales? You think you can say anything to me. You think you can make people do exactly what you want, that you can play the spy, then tell everybody what to do, how to live. That is what you think, isn't it? Well isn't it?"

"It's for you, only for you," I cried. "I had to tell you. If you hide things, never talk about things, they come out, out in other ways." I shook my head; I knew I wasn't saying it right. She'd never understand. And I couldn't do it any better.

My mother gave a slight laugh, suddenly. "Lord, children are something else. Who would believe it? Your father works hard for us. He brings home every penny. Some men gamble. Some drink. Some beat up their wives and kids. Have you heard about any of this, Inky? Have you thought about that, since you're so eager to find fault?"

"I—I—I'm not trying to find fault, Mom. Honest. I love him. I love you."

"Love?" Again, that laugh, slight and harsh. "Ingrid, you know nothing about love. Love doesn't destroy. Love doesn't accuse. Ingrid, listen to me. I will never discuss this with you again. Ingrid, a marriage is a sacred pact between two people. Nobody, nobody else in the world has any business interfering in that pact. Do you understand?"

My mother got up from the sofa. She went to the window and drew the drapes, then locked the front door as she always did at night.

I sat there limp, as if I were a stuffed toy, placed there, unable to move on my own.

"One more thing, Inky," my mother said. She had turned off the light, and I saw her now in the shadows, her eyes glistening, face soft and round, like a moon. "Don't for one moment even consider speaking to your father about this. Don't even imagine it. It would destroy—"

For a long moment she held the pause, while together we held the thought . . . what? What would be destroyed?

"Everything," she said.

16

It's a weird thing, how I slept that night. Like a log. And one crazy thought kept on turning through my mind: I did not destroy the world. No. I am not the destroyer of the world. And then in my dream I was flying over the big Ficus tree and I saw a little bird hop over to the edge of a nest. It looked down, and began to dance to a rockabilly band! I woke up laughing. I sat up in bed. Then I remembered, and I cried.

In the morning I took my bike and went down to the pool, where we had swum all summer. It was deserted now, except for old Hank Potter who fixes things and keeps kids from getting too rowdy. The gate to the pool was locked.

"Could I get into the pool, please, Hank?"

He looked up at me, scratching his grizzled head.

"You want to go swimming? Pool doesn't open until noon today. You know that. Winter schedule."

"I'm not going swimming," I said, smiling at him. "I just want to climb the ladder to the high dive."

He scratched his head again, dubious. This was not in his instructions. "I'm not supposed to let anyone go in there *swimming*," he defined.

"That's right. Nobody ever said anything about climbing the ladder, did they? You could come with me," I suggested. "See that I don't hurt anything."

"Yup. Well, I suppose I could." He got out his keys, paused in the midst of unlocking the gate. He pushed it open, then asked, "Why would you want to get up on that ladder, though, if you don't aim to dive into the pool?"

I smiled again. "Oh, just a little bet I have with someone."

"A bet?" Old Hank Potter looked around to establish some companion waiting beyond the bushes. "With who?"

I laughed. "With myself, Hank. Me. Ingrid Stevenson, world class aerialist, balloonist, sky diver. Me."

IT WASN'T EASY climbing up on that ladder. I spent an hour there at the pool. I went all the way up. Once, twice, three times, holding onto the rungs so tight that my fingers ached. By the sixth time I was soaked with sweat. I relaxed my grip just a little on the rungs. The eighth time, when I got to the top, I opened my eyes. I looked down at the water. And as I held my stance there on the high diving board, I noticed that I could look out across town to the mall, over to Lankersheim's dairy, clear to the low hills, and for an instant I thought I even spotted a dot of red, blue, and yellow, bobbing in the distance.

Hank, watching from below, dourly twisted his lip.

"How many more times you gonna do that? Ain't you getting tired?"

"Just twice more," I said.

"This some kind of a new way to lose weight?" he asked.

"Yeah," I said with a grin. "I was getting really weighted down, Hank. But not with fat, you see."

"Huh?"

I laughed. Fears can weigh very heavy, I thought.

THE REST OF THAT DAY I spent on homework. I usually keep up with my studies. Now, algebra pages fluttered around me, undone. I set to work. All afternoon I worked on problems. In the evening I finished that novel Mrs. Ebert had been pestering me about. It wasn't bad. Not bad at all, in fact. It was two in the morning when I finished, tired and oddly happy. I had work to do. Things to accomplish. I felt as if I'd been on a strange journey, outside my own skin, and now I was back.

Monday at school Caroline and I talked. It was lunchtime, and we wandered out to the trees where we could be alone.

"I'm going to go up in that balloon," I told her. "I'm going to do it if it kills me."

"Will your mom let you?"

"I'm not telling her."

"How can you keep secrets from your mother that way? I never could. I mean, my mom just knows what I'm thinking, almost."

I shrugged. "People are different. You and your folks like to talk about everything. Mine don't."

"Did you . . . did you ever talk to your mom? You know, about those letters?"

"Yes. I talked to her. I tried."

"What did she say? What's she going to do? Inky, did she cry? My mom would. She'd be so upset."

"Caroline," I said softly, "my mom isn't like yours. Not at all. She told me—well, she told me things. About marriage. It's a sacred pact, she said. It's between them."

"Are you going to tell your father?"

"No. Never. It wouldn't be right." I said nothing more, and neither did Caroline. She only nodded. Then she said, "Want to come over this afternoon and do our nails?" That's the terrific thing about Caroline. She doesn't insist.

"I can't. I've got all these homework assignments to make up. And then I've got to make that poster for the McMurphys."

By the end of the week I had finished my back assignments, and I was ready to do the poster in paints. I didn't know how I'd deliver it. Certainly not on my bike.

Maybe Caroline's mom would take me in her car. I decided not to worry about it. I'd find a way.

I told Grandma that afternoon I was going to Mc-Clure's for some art supplies. "Do you want anything?"

"Well, yes, you could get me a crafts magazine. I heard from Midge Greeley they have a new one on quilts, would you mind? Ask for the *Abracadabra Quilting and Knitting*, this month's issue. Run to my room, dear, and get two dollars from my black purse."

"Where's Mom?"

"She's resting. Her back . . . ."

I went into Grandma's room, into the strange fragrance of cushions and plants and yarn and the cinnamon tea she likes so much. I stood there listening. I heard the sound of her chopping vegetables in the kitchen. Certainly, she had heard everything from here. Yet she kept silent. She could not risk hearing too much.

Grandma had told me, "I will always have a home here with my son." I caught a glimpse now, of the fear that lay behind those words. Suppose she didn't have us? Where would she go? How could she survive?

I took the money from her purse, remembering how she looked for her Social Security check each month.

"I'm a lucky woman, Ingrid. Your father has taken me into his house to live, your mother takes good care of me, and Uncle Sam sends me a little spending money each month. What more could I want?"

Mother did take good care of Grandma. She never left her alone. She fixed all her meals and changed her bed linen and sat with her in the late afternoons. How often Mother explained, not really complaining but letting us know, that taking care of the house and of Grandma hardly left her time for anything else. They needed each other.

Dad was coming home that night. As if it had already happened, I knew exactly how it would be. "Mail call!" He'd be jovial and beaming. Bringing presents. I would hear him singing in the shower, "Home, home on the range!"

"How was everything, Marguerite?"

"Just fine, Peter. Nothing new."

"I asked about those international flights. Too much hassle. I'd need different certification, a different airline, maybe lose seniority. I just get a little restless sometimes, Marguerite."

"I know, Peter. I understand." And he would hand her a box containing something pretty, something new for her to wear at suppertime.

As I rode to McClure's, I thought about Gus, the way he told me everything, the way he and his mother looked for truth. Something was missing in my family. I knew that, and it hurt. But I got a new thought, too. Gus had said it. People can decide how they want to be. They can work on it. Maybe if my mom had had someone like Gus to talk to, I thought, she wouldn't be hidden away in the house now.

I pulled my bike to the stand in front of McClures.

linen and sat with her in the late afternoons. How often Mother explained, not really complaining but letting us know, that taking care of the house and of Grandma hardly left her time for anything else. They needed each other.

Dad was coming home that night. As if it had already happened, I knew exactly how it would be. "Mail call!" He'd be jovial and beaming. Bringing presents. I would hear him singing in the shower, "Home, home on the range!"

"How was everything, Marguerite?"

"Just fine, Peter. Nothing new."

"I asked about those international flights. Too much hassle. I'd need different certification, a different airline, maybe lose seniority. I just get a little restless sometimes, Marguerite."

"I know, Peter. I understand." And he would hand her a box containing something pretty, something new for her to wear at suppertime.

As I rode to McClure's, I thought about Gus, the way he told me everything, the way he and his mother looked for truth. Something was missing in my family. I knew that, and it hurt. But I got a new thought, too. Gus had said it. People can decide how they want to be. They can work on it. Maybe if my mom had had someone like Gus to talk to, I thought, she wouldn't be hidden away in the house now.

I pulled my bike to the stand in front of McClures.

Maybe Caroline's mom would take me in her car. I decided not to worry about it. I'd find a way.

I told Grandma that afternoon I was going to McClure's for some art supplies. "Do you want anything?"

"Well, yes, you could get me a crafts magazine. I heard from Midge Greeley they have a new one on quilts, would you mind? Ask for the *Abracadabra Quilting and Knitting*, this month's issue. Run to my room, dear, and get two dollars from my black purse."

"Where's Mom?"

"She's resting. Her back . . . ."

I went into Grandma's room, into the strange fragrance of cushions and plants and yarn and the cinnamon tea she likes so much. I stood there listening. I heard the sound of her chopping vegetables in the kitchen. Certainly, she had heard everything from here. Yet she kept silent. She could not risk hearing too much.

Grandma had told me, "I will always have a home here with my son." I caught a glimpse now, of the fear that lay behind those words. Suppose she didn't have us? Where would she go? How could she survive?

I took the money from her purse, remembering how she looked for her Social Security check each month.

"I'm a lucky woman, Ingrid. Your father has taken me into his house to live, your mother takes good care of me, and Uncle Sam sends me a little spending money each month. What more could I want?"

Mother did take good care of Grandma. She never left her alone. She fixed all her meals and changed her bed

She nodded. "Mind if I start? I can hardly wait. Say, how about sharing this with me? I had no idea they were so large."

Hot fudge sundaes are my absolute favorite. I eyed hers, my mouth watering.

"I could order one of my own," I said politely.

"Let's finish this one first. If we're still hungry, we'll order another."

"Terrific!"

We dug in, loving it. Mary McMurphy looked up, smiling. "I like your hair that way. It's cute. Frames your face."

"Thanks."

We took turns dipping in our spoons. I remarked, "The only other person I've ever shared a sundae with is Becca. My little sister."

"Do you mind eating from the same dish? You don't think it's gross?"

"Not at all," I said. "That is, when you're friends."

She nodded. "Mmm. This is fabulous. But I'm stuffed. You want the rest?"

I shook my head. "My eyes are always more ambitious than the rest of me."

"A common situation," said Mary McMurphy. "I've gotten into a heap of trouble because of that. Like the balloon. I thought it would be simple. Just a little old balloon. Of course, then comes the basket, then the instruments, then the truck to carry it in, and insurance, et cetera, et cetera."

Inside, I browsed through the wide aisles, looking at all the wares. I chose three jars of poster paints, red, blue and yellow, a wide brush and a thick black felt pen, already imagining my handiwork. I love to paint.

Near the cash registers I saw the rack with its many crafts magazines, and I readily found the one Grandma wanted, with the picture of a hand knitted afghan on the cover.

I paid for my purchases and went out to Peaches Ice Cream Store, wondering if this time I should have something different. Maybe English toffee. Maybe praline coconut. Why not?

As I entered, I confronted my reflection in the plate glass window, and I remembered Grandma's praise of my looks. Not too bad, I acknowledged now, eyeing my pink sweater and pale blue denims. I had not tied back my hair this morning, but left it to curl. Not bad, I thought, as if that face belonged to another girl, one who looked pretty good in curls.

"What a nice surprise!"

I peered beyond the counter to the tables and chairs in the ice cream shop. There sat Mrs. McMurphy, in front of a hot fudge sundae.

She smiled. "Ingrid, I'm so glad to see you. I hate making a pig of myself all alone. Sit down. We'll have a party. I've missed you."

"Well, I've had a lot of catching up to do," I said. "Homework and stuff."

"It becomes a way of life," I said solemnly.

"Exactly."

"What will you do when Gus leaves?"

"Well, Josh, the young man who delivers the mail, has been working at getting a pilot's license. Two can really manage it; three is much better. Maybe," she said with a penetrating look at me, "we'll find another assistant."

I pretended not to notice her obvious offer. Me, helping with a balloon launch? Apparently Gus had not told her about our talk.

"I got some poster paints," I said, "for your project. I'm going to start it today. It should be finished by the weekend."

As I reached into the bag to show Mrs. McMurphy the poster paints, the magazine slid out. Mrs. McMurphy's keen eyes saw the cover and she asked, "Are you making an afghan, too?"

"No, not I. This is for my . . . ."

Instantly my knees turned to jelly. I could have lied and said the magazine was for our housekeeper. Instead I answered, "Mrs. McMurphy, the magazine is for my grandma." I took a deep breath. "She lives with us. With me and my father and Becca and . . . ." I looked up at her. "My mother."

I felt hot all over with shame, and I was trembling. It was the hardest thing I had ever done, to tell her. If I'd thought it over, I'd never have been able to do it. Sometimes, I guess, you just have to jump in.

Mrs. McMurphy didn't say anything for a while. She only stared at me. Then, with a slight smile and a nod she said, "I see. Yes. I see," as if she had wondered about something, and now it was settled.

"Are you going to tell Gus?"

"What would I tell him?" she asked.

"That I lied all this time. That my mother's not dead."

"It's not up to me to tell him that."

"You won't say anything?"

"Why would I?"

"Because—because you wouldn't want me to see him again, would you?"

"Why?" She stared at me, her mouth wide with incredulity. "Because you don't always tell the truth? Because you aren't perfect? Because something upset you so much that you had to pretend, and the pretense became a permanent pose? Ingrid, I know about that. Oh, don't I know it," she said with a low sound. "I lived with a lie for fourteen years. Apparently it's only taken you a few months to wake up."

"I—I—I wouldn't want Gus to think that everything I ever told him was a lie. About myself, I mean, about—I don't know what to say."

Mary McMurphy shook her head, and her hair fell about her shoulders. "Just tell him the truth, Ingrid."

"Sometimes the truth doesn't work!" I cried. "Some people don't want to hear the truth." Something exploded in me, a million tears, regrets, longings.

"You can only try your best," she replied softly. "Ingrid, there aren't any guarantees."

"Don't you want to know why I did it?"

"I know why."

"How could you?" I breathed.

"You were unhappy," she said. "You didn't like the world the way you found it. So you invented a new one for yourself." Mary McMurphy chuckled. "We all do that to some extent. You just did it in spades."

"Yeah!" I laughed now, too. "I did. Killed people off, made them vanish."

A gesture of Mrs. McMurphy's, a certain expression, sent us both into peals of laughter, strange laughter but loud and free, born of the huge relief I felt, and of her understanding.

Patrons in the ice cream store looked at us. They must have thought we were mother and daughter, having a good time together.

In a way, I thought, we were.

17

THAT NIGHT I sat at the kitchen table with my poster board and paints, the bright colors flowing into the design I had at last created. Becca was braiding a lanyard from plastic strips left over from summer day camp. My parents were in their room; I could hear their voices dimly. I wondered: What do they talk about?

I was concentrating so hard that I didn't hear them approach.

"Our artist," said my father. "That's gorgeous, Inky."

"Thanks."

"Something for school?" my mother asked.

"A contest?" Grandma added, smiling. "You're sure to win, Inky. That's beautiful. I don't know how you do it."

I glanced at Becca. She kept her face deadpan. She was getting to be very good at that sort of thing.

"It's not for school," I said. That strange sense of heaviness was upon me again, the choking feeling, the same as when that Roadrunner headdress came down on my head—the scared-to-death feeling that I wanted to run from. But I grasped the edge of the table, hanging on, and I said, "It's for a friend."

"Oh?" My mother's eyes were wide. "Someone we know?"

"Now, Marguerite," said my father with a slight smile, "we don't need to pry. Inky has her own friends."

"It's all right," I said, though my pulse throbbed and I felt as if they were all crowding in on me. "I have a friend who lives out at Shea Station."

"A man?" my mother asked. "Are you telling us you have been associating with a man who lives out in the desert?"

"Marguerite, Inky is almost in high school. We must give her some freedom."

"Well, whoever said she isn't free?" my mother cried, her cheeks red now, eyes blazing. "You talk as if I keep her prisoner, Peter! Inky can do what she likes. As for me, I wouldn't be caught dead out in the desert on a bicycle. What if she got a flat tire?"

"Mom!" I cried. "Listen. Please. He's eighteen," I said, moistening my lips. "He and his mom run the balloon launch. I've visited the launch. Lots of times. He's a nice boy. We're always there with his mother. She does typing for people, and she bakes her own bread, and makes soup and . . . she's a nice lady. She likes me. She asked me to make a poster for them. This is it."

"The balloon launch? Out in the desert? Hot air balloons?" My mother's incredulous look placed hot air balloons in the same category as flying saucers. "I've heard those things can explode. I wouldn't get near one of those things."

"They've invited me to go up," I said

"What?" My mother let out a laugh. It grew, cascading upward, until her face was screwed up with laughter, her cheeks red and damp from laughing tears. "Oh, Lord, I can just see it, you'll never get off the ground. You'll be so scared, you'll probably wet your pants."

Grandma murmured something about her TV show and left. My father stood gazing at me. "Are you serious about this, Inky?"

"I'd like to try it," I said. "Will you let me?"

"No," he said. "But I won't stop you, either. You have to earn your own way," he said. "Take your own risks. If something goes wrong, you have to be ready to face the consequences."

I stared at my father now. He looked neither handsome nor playful, but tired and a little concerned.

"I don't have to worry," Mom said with a sniff. "I know my daughter."

* * *

I SPENT most of the weekend at the old pool. I swam. I even jumped off the diving board into the water. The high dive came next. Some of the kids from school were there; I wished one of them had been Buzz. I might have told him I was sorry for that punch in the stomach. But Buzz wasn't there, and the kids who were didn't pay any attention to the fact that I was jumping from the high dive. They completely ignored me, as if jumping ten feet into the pool was something that's done every day.

By Wednesday I had gotten up the courage to go out to the launch. I didn't know exactly what I'd say to Gus. But I knew I'd ask him to come to my house and get the poster. From there, it was all ad lib.

Gus was in the front yard, leaning on a spade, resting from the effort of digging out a dead eucalyptus tree. The roots must have gone deep and far; sweat beaded on his face and stained his shirt.

He saw me, looked down, then nodded. Something had happened. Things were different, not only with me, but on his part.

"Hi there," he said, without intonation or the usual grin.

"Hi." I put down my bike. "What are you doing?"

"Digging to China," he said flatly.

"Very funny." I saw his face, that thunderous look. "What's wrong?"

"You can see I'm busy," he said.

"Gus. Can't you stop for a minute?"

He grunted, continued digging. I wanted to scream

at him. I wanted to hate him. Whoever the girl was in Tucson, she could have him!

I picked up my bike. I let it roll slowly toward the driveway. Men, I thought. All alike. *Disgusting.*

But something made me turn back. I walked my bike up to where he stood. "I guess your mom told you," I said. "That's why I came today. I wanted to explain."

"Nothing to explain. She told me, all right."

"She said she wouldn't!" I cried.

"I forced her. I was going to go over to your house. I wondered why we hadn't seen you. I was on the way. She stopped me. Told me it would only upset and embarrass you. That she'd met you at the ice cream store, and you told her you lived with your parents. *Two* parents. Mother and father. Even a grandmother to boot. What a jerk I was."

"A—a jerk?" I could not see clearly. A film rose before my eyes; I could not think what it was, tried to brush it away, found it impossible.

"Oh, yeah, the world's prize nerd. Telling you all this stuff, thinking you'd really understand, having been through it yourself. I tried talking once to a boy who was my friend. Supposed to be my friend. I found out, until people have felt something themselves, they—they wear sort of a shield. They don't feel things. For sure, they don't understand. When my friend found out my dad had died, he said, 'Oh, well, he was sick, wasn't he?' As if that made it O.K. After that, I just didn't talk about it."

"You said you talked at Al-anon."

"That was different. That was the group."

"What makes you think I have to have a parent die to know how you feel?"

"Because if you really knew, you wouldn't lie about something like death. Not something like that."

"Your mother didn't see it that way."

"My mother is not me. It's not the same. I never held out on you. I don't appreciate it when people do that to me. Listen, I've got to go. I have lots of studying to do. My course work is due. Maybe I'll see you some time."

He thrust the spade into the ground and turned, taking long strides to the porch and then two steps up at a time. He went in and slammed the door, probably certain that I would ride away. But I didn't.

I picked up the spade. I dug. And as I dug, I realized that the film before my eyes was nothing but tears. Go ahead! I screamed to myself. *Go ahead, cry, you idiot, but you're not going to run away!* I threw my weight onto the spade, feeling its sharp metallic bite against the sole of my foot, and I dug down deep and brought out a great clod of earth, so heavy that I had to strain back with all my might to raise it. Straining, grunting, the tears still falling, I heaved it up, tossed it over to the left, then dug in again. Roots tore loose with a cracking sound, hung out like long, spikey fingers. *Out! Out!* I silently screamed, thinking of all the lies I had told, lies no different from those of my father. I dug deeper, deeper, until the earth changed color from black to a strange ochre, and I saw layers upon layers of soil. *Out! Out!* And I thought of all the layers of self deception my poor mother had practiced all these years, never meeting problems, hiding her feelings, never forgiving. *I'm not going to be like that!*

I dug until my arms and shoulders ached. Then I stormed up the steps of the porch and pounded on the door.

Annie barked.

"Go see who that is, Gus!" Mrs. McMurphy yelled over her typing.

Gus flung open the door. He stared at me, aghast. He seemed about to slam the door shut again, but I thrust out my foot and yelled, "Gus! I'm coming in there to talk to you. Get out of the doorway, I'm coming in!"

He stepped aside, and as I hurled my way past him, I felt the blow of my side against his arm, hard enough to bruise. I yelled, "Ow!" and doubled up my fists, ready to belt him one, make him fight, and then, finally, forgive.

WE TALKED. The typing continued. Eventually Mrs. McMurphy came in with mugs of hot Ovaltine. "Soothing to the nerves," she said with a smile at me. She knew. No secrets here. The doors were kept open.

I avoided his gaze at first, then was able to look at Gus straight on, concluding, "So the more I lied, the deeper it got. Like a game at first. After a while, there was too much to unravel. And I wanted you to think I was . . ." I sighed deeply, "O.K."

"You are O.K.," Gus finally said, his voice very low. "You just made a mistake." He frowned. "I just don't understand why. Why would you tell me your mother was dead? And all that stuff about having to stay home and take care of your sister?"

I shook my head. "Maybe, in a way, I wanted things to be a lot simpler than they are. If it was just me and my dad . . . ." I shook my head. "Gus, I can't tell you everything. It's personal, to me and my family. It's just that . . . we have some problems. Maybe someday I can tell people. But not now. Now I'm just going to . . . ." I stood up, my arms wide, and took a deep breath, like a new beginning, "I'm going to start doing things differently."

Gus stood up, too. "Like what?"

"Like inviting you to Seven Wells," I said. "I made that poster for you. You'll have to come and pick it up. I can't bring it on my bike."

"When's a good time?" he asked.

"How about now?"

"You're on!"

"Don't know why they call it Seven Wells," I told Gus as we rode along, my bike in back of the truck. "I've only found three of them."

"Someone probably thought seven sounded luckier," Gus said.

"Simple, huh?"

"Why not?"

"I'd like for you to meet my little sister."

"Why don't you bring her to the launch sometime?"

"How would she get there? It's too far for her to bike."

"How do you know?"

"She's only ten."

"Ingrid, give the kid a little credit. Ten isn't that young."

We pulled up, as I pointed, in front of my house. It looked sealed, small, ordinary.

"I'll go get the poster."

I ran in, brought out the poster and handed it to Gus. He gave a whistle of approval. "Mighty nice," he said. "My mom will love it. Don't forget, we pay our debts, one hot air balloon ride, upon request."

"Gus." I gazed at him. "Don't count on it. I'm trying, but . . . ." I tried to smile. "My mother says hot air balloons can blow up."

Gus eyed me seriously. "Accidents can happen," he admitted. "There are risks in ballooning. You could hit a sudden wind, or touch a power line. The balloon could catch fire while you're firing up, if you aren't careful. I can't give you any guarantees, Ingrid, except that we follow all the regulations, and it's always safety first."

"I'm really trying, Gus," I said, though my voice shook as I envisioned disasters based on my mother's warning. I recalled other warnings: Don't swim in the ocean, stay away from the cages at the zoo, don't eat foreign foods, don't run across the street. Some of them were sensible, others were silly. I'd have to decide which was which.

"It doesn't matter, Ingrid," Gus said gently. "Even if you never go up, it's O.K."

"It matters to me," I told him fiercely. "I hate being a wimp."

"You're no wimp," Gus said, and gently he kissed me.

18

"I DON'T THINK you should lie to your friends," I told Becca. We were sitting on my bed, arguing.

"You told me to in the first place."

"I was wrong."

"It's just a little white lie." Becca blew onto her nails; she had painted them with clear gloss. "No harm. It will be easier."

"For whom?"

"I don't want them to yell at me! They'll call me chicken. They'll think I don't want to hang around with them, but I do, Inky. Tina and Nonie and I are best friends. They'll go to practice almost every day after school, and Saturdays they'll be with the team, and I'll be out of it."

"Then play."

"I can't!"

"Why not?"

"I don't know why."

"Yes, you do."

"I don't!"

"You said you're a lousy athlete. How can you get better if you never try? What are you afraid of?"

Becca started to cry. No puckering, no warning, just those slow tears. "I don't want to get hit in the mouth. Mom says soccer is dangerous."

"Becca. How many girls do you know who have had their teeth knocked out with a soccer ball?" She didn't answer. I poked her. "How many?"

"None. But there's always a first time."

"You don't make any sense. And you miss a lot of fun being scared of everything."

"I'm not scared of everything. Just of getting hurt."

"That's ridiculous," I snapped.

"No more ridiculous than you," Becca shouted. "You're even afraid to go up on the roof. I always go up on the roof to help Daddy clean out the gutters, and that's really dangerous."

"I can go on the roof," I said. Already, my hands felt sweaty, and the back of my neck prickled. "I can go anywhere I want. I can even go up in a balloon."

"Are you kidding? You'd be petrified."

"I can do it."

"You're crazy. Mom wouldn't let you."

"She never said I couldn't. She thought I'd be too scared."

Becca sat very still, her arms wrapped tightly around herself.

"Becca," I said gently, taking her hand, "it's O.K. to be scared. Everyone is scared of some things. But you have to make yourself try, anyhow. Or else you get worse and worse, and pretty soon you won't try anything, but just sit home being scared. Like . . . ." I bit my lip. "Like soccer," I said. "It's a chance for you to try something new. Go with your friends, Becca. I'll bet when you do it, you'll feel terrific. You don't have to play goalie. They're the ones that get it in the teeth. You can just be a forward or a guard. I'll practice with you, Becca, and I'll come to your games and cheer."

"It's easy for you to say it," Becca said. "I don't feel well."

"What's wrong now?"

"I have a stomachache. Leave me alone, Inky. I don't want to talk about it anymore, I just want to be left alone. I have a headache."

I took a hard look at her and said firmly, "Becca, I'm going to do it. I'm going to go up in that balloon."

"I don't believe you."

"Wait and see."

"You won't do it. You'll chicken out at the last minute. I bet you won't."

"Be ready to get up at dawn," I told her. "I'm taking you with me. I'll show you."

DAWN IN THE DESERT is a special time. The morning chill hugs the ground and creeps out from the hills, blending into the color purple. The sage is stiff and still, and the sound of bike wheels on asphalt is as crisp as skis on new snow. Desert birds are active in early morning, and great balls of tumbleweed roll over the ground, gathering speed and size as they go.

Becca and I rode without speaking. I was conscious of her breathing, but I kept up my pace. She did not complain; somehow Becca understood that this ride was a test. Earlier, at home, while we silently pulled on our clothes and crept out the door, she asked, "Is it far? How many miles? What if I can't make it?"

"It's your decision," I told her then, sharply. "No guarantees. Are you coming or not?"

She wavered only for a moment, then got out her bike. As we neared the launch, two trucks and a van passed us. They were filled with balloonists, judging by the anticipation on their faces, and the bulky bundles they carried: Helmets, gloves, ropes, burners, baskets, and, of course, the balloon packed in its envelope. It was as if an entirely different civilization existed here, at dawn, while others—pity them!—were still sleeping.

I wasn't scared now. That had been dealt with in the night. For hours I laid awake, terrified at the hundreds of dangers that might await me in the morning. The balloon could burn up, hit a power pole, crash into a tree. I might actually die of fright, or scream out in panic, or, worse, have what my mother used to call "an accident."

The alarm under my pillow had gone off at 5:00 AM. I was instantly awake, moving mechanically, briskly. No thoughts, no feelings were left, only that sense of movement, duty, like a soldier.

Now, as we neared the launch site and looked down, the people appeared smaller, especially against the enormous balloon that lay stretched out flat on the ground. The colors were vivid in the early desert light, the cables and ropes and baskets littered the broad fields like the peculiar paraphernalia of an alien race.

"Inky!" Becca shrieked with excitement. We walked our bikes the rest of the way. It seemed wrong to rush in; we stood at the edge for a few moments, watching, listening. We had worn our padded jackets, for it was cold, and now we clapped our hands together to warm them, watching the people in the distance doing the same, reaching for thermoses of hot coffee and cider. Steam rose from their breath and from the hot drinks, the vapor mingling with the steely gray atmosphere that hovers over the desert at dawn's edge.

As we drew closer, the scene came alive, the people larger, alert, excited. You could tell who was crew; they moved with long, sure strides, taking care, taking charge. You could tell who were passengers, with their expressions of expectation. It was that look of being about to do something magnificent, something for the first time, because for a balloonist, I'd been told, each time is a first, each time supreme; the thrill never wanes.

Noise, more than anything, accosted us. The noise of huge fans pushing air into the balloons, the underlying sound of the propane being fired and flowing into burners; the orders being shouted to ground crews: "Watch that line! Hands off now, a moment . . . . Back, pull back on the skirt! Get out of the way, you. Inspected that line? Get some gloves on, hurry! Hey, get that truck out of there . . . ."

I saw Gus at the same moment that he noticed me and Becca standing at the edge of the small crowd. About forty or fifty people were there in all, some ground crew, some pilots, some passengers, and most of them spectators.

"Ingrid!" Gus ran up to me, his arms out to give me a squeeze, fast and furious, so that I gasped, laughing, swallowing my fear once and for all. "You'll go up? Great. I want you to take first launch. Who's this? Must be Rebecca. Hi, Becca. Listen, you can ride in the truck with my mom to meet the balloon. Hey, come over here with me, Ingrid; I've got to go. Josh is holding my place . . . don't be scared. It's just a lot of noise. Can't hurt you. Hold onto me. It'll be just like I told you."

He led me to a pile of clothes, gave me a yellow helmet and a pair of gloves. "The gloves are just for show," he said, grinning. "Makes you look official, like crew. Keep

that helmet on. Josh! Listen, you stay down the first time.
I'm taking Ingrid up. You can take the second ride; think
you can direct the ground crew? Great." All this was
shouted out, and I stood there watching, bewildered,
aware that I felt nothing, that my body was given up to
this noise and commotion and action, to flame and wind
and the swelling, straining, bobbing balloon; if something happened, if disaster did strike, even if I died this
day, it didn't matter. I thought of the ancient Indian
saying, that Mrs. Ebert had told us about in class, "It is
a good day to die," and as I repeated those words in my
mind I began to laugh, first inside, and then out loud.

"Passengers!"

Somehow I was pushed, lifted, tumbled into the basket, and beside me was Gus and a man and his wife, the
four of us squeezed together, now being given instructions: Hold on to the sides of the basket, no sitting down,
face the direction of landing, stay away from the red
cord . . . don't touch. Don't touch.

A fury of noise seemed to lift us in its own power.
"Hands off!"

I had expected a lurch, a jolt. What I felt was similar
to rising up from the bottom of a pool, rising swiftly,
effortlessly, rising to meet sunlight and rippling shadows.
I must have been numb with emotion; my body seemed
not to exist, nor, really, my mind. Something else took
over. Maybe that something is what they call spirit or
soul; I only know that every ounce of fear and dread and
sadness flowed out of me the instant we were aloft.

Gradually I became aware that the noise was incredible, that Gus was a virtual demon of energy and concentration, watching the instruments, controlling the flame, heating the air so that we continued to rise, rise, rise. Then, suddenly, Gus closed the valve. Silence reigned.

"Oh!" cried the woman. Her husband smiled. "It's so quiet!"

I said nothing, but looked up, following where Gus pointed, to the interior of the huge balloon rising over our heads, and it was like being inside a cathedral entirely made of stained glass, a round, protective, womb-like shrine that glowed with sun-filled colors of red, yellow, and blue. The sun was rising swiftly, spreading light and color over the sky; I felt that we were at the center of the sunrise.

We floated. I can't say for how long. It doesn't matter. Perfect moments need no clock. I saw colors and flowing shapes, felt currents and exotic breezes, heard my own voice as a marvel never before experienced. "It's heaven," I whispered to Gus.

"Of course," he whispered back. "No way to describe it. But now you know."

Business again, action, pulling the cord to let out the hot air, to make the descent, moving with the wind sideways, a little faster—too fast! Heat again, the noise engulfing us, drowning us, the balloon now rising swift and with a jolt, the calamitous power lines looking far too close though they were a quarter of a mile away. And then the sure and swift downward pull, with treetops approaching, dogs barking, houses with pointed roofs and chimneys suddenly thrusting up at us, approaching, approaching, and then I felt a twinge of fear—but just a twinge—for I saw Gus maneuvering it with firm, steady, skilled determination. "Lean toward the fall!" he shouted. A jolt. A bump. Dragging and bumping along the field, the hard soil jolting us the more in comparison to the free, sweet, airborne existence we had too briefly known.

"Ah!" Sounds, only, no words. Then, "How long were we up?"

"Half an hour."

"What? Impossible. It seemed like just five minutes."

"That's it, sir. The beginning of the bug. It never feels long enough. Now you know."

Gus was talking to the man, but looking at me.

In the minutes that followed, Gus was busy giving orders, helping us climb out and showing us how to hold down the balloon as we waited for the chase vehicles. The truck with the next load of passengers rolled toward us with Mrs. McMurphy at the wheel.

Becca jumped out and ran ahead toward me, squealing, shouting my name. "Inky! Inky! You really did it!" Her eyes were moist, glowing.

We who had already ridden changed places with the next line of passengers; I released my hold on the basket, gave Gus a look that was more than a smile, which he returned in kind.

Becca leaped and giggled at my side. I threw open my arms, gathered her in. "Oh, Becca," I sighed.

"What was it like?"

"It was—awesome," I said, using her word. I laughed slightly. "Like seeing a unicorn."

Becca made a face. "Oh, unicorns." She took my hand, held it tightly. "Ink, if I tell you something, promise you won't tell Daddy?"

"What is it?"

"I don't really believe in unicorns anymore. I don't know when I quit. But Daddy loves to pretend about it."

"I'll be our secret," I said, giving her a quick hug.

Gus and Josh and the other riders waved to us as the balloon once more started to rise.

"Happy landings!" shouted Mrs. McMurphy. She called to me and Becca. "Come on! Don't you want to meet them when they land?"

"We can't," said Becca. "We'd better get home."

I drew back, puzzled. "Why can't we stay?"

"I have to be at the park by nine. Soccer." She gave a small, embarrassed smile. "If you can go ballooning, I guess I can kick a little old ball around, at least I can try it. And if I like it," she added hastily, "I'll have to buy a soccer ball and practice in the yard, and I'll get a soccer shirt and special shoes, and you and I can play together every evening."

"Quite a switch," I said, grinning, "from unicorns to soccer. Well, I guess there is a season for everything.

Come on, then. Let's go back to the launch. We've got a long ride home."

For a minute or so, as we ran along the road back to the launch, the balloon hovered overhead, casting its shadow upon us, like a gentle caress. Then it was gone, and the bright sun overhead signaled a new day.